Pack Dreams

A NEW ADULT PARANORMAL ROMANCE

MIDNIGHT WOLVES OF SMOKY FALLS
BOOK ONE

LAUREL NIGHT

Important Note!

This is an updated, rewritten, and completely re-edited version of Pack Dreams.

Thanks to feedback from readers, I decided to make some changes that will hopefully improve the overall feel and excitement of the story.

None of the plot has changed, but I've added in some more moments, feelings, and all-around emotion to the story. I hope you enjoy this new, slightly sexier (but still slow burn!) version.

Cheers!
Laurel

Author's Note

Dear reader,

Thanks for picking up this book. I really hope you enjoy exploring Layla's mysterious new world and diving into the secrets of Smoky Falls.

It's important that you know - this book is slow burn. I set out to write something spicier out the gate, but it didn't fit the characters in the end, and I had to follow what the characters wanted.

This is a New Adult, friends-to-lovers romance. If you enjoy The Veil Diaries, you should expect that level of steam from the first book. I promise it will become spicier in book 2, Pack Nightmare, and then the heat really comes in book 3, Dawn of the Pack. But for now have patience and give Layla a chance to show you why Smoky Falls is an amazing place.

If you don't have patience for slow burn, then this book may not be for you, and that's 100% okay. :)

If you're here for the slow burn, then read on and enjoy, my friend!

Cheers,

Laurel

Chapter One

LAYLA

∼

No one even knew I existed until the story of an unknown girl being viciously attacked on the street made national news. It turned out my legal name was Lilliana Harridan, although my parents always called me Layla Harris.

Since I ran away from the foster home four years ago, I've just gone by Lex. That is, until my mysterious uncle claimed me after the attack and set me up with a caretaker in LA, while I finished physical therapy and caught up in school. With so many mysteries and so few answers in the year since my attack, I can't wait to reach my uncle's house and start diving into my family's history.

In my mind, my uncle is a dark shadowy figure, like

the beast in his castle. Apparently, he's the mayor of Smoky Falls, so he has to remain in town to run things. In the last year, we haven't even talked on video chat; I occasionally get one short, growly phone call to update him on my progress.

Roxanne came to take care of me but works for my uncle, and always makes apologies he's busy. For the long-lost niece he was so happy to discover, it certainly feels like I can't matter that much to him if I barely merit a five-minute phone call once a month.

Now, of course, I'm finally about to meet the legend himself. My chauffeur-driven SUV is cruising through the dense forest of the Smoky Mountains. Even after all this time, I miss Derrek and my friends. My street family. My memories of the attack are still murky, but I know Derrek found me and scared off my attacker. I never got to thank him, or even say goodbye. The guilt swims in my chest like a living thing as I stare out the window at passing trees.

I rub my forearms subconsciously. The deep cuts have long since healed, and the scars have faded, but they still itch sometimes. Dr. Rosen assures me it's a psychological response, not a physical one. Even so, I swear I feel something from time to time, like nails raking over my skin, and it sends shivers down my spine. I only have flashes of memory from that night, no real detail to haunt my dreams, and for that I'm grateful.

Pulling the sleeves of my oversized sweater down to completely envelop my hands, I think about what

Roxanne told me. From what she says, I get the impression my uncle has a big house, but both she and Dr. Rosen have been incredibly vague whenever I ask questions about anything related to Smoky Falls. At first, their tight-lipped tendencies pissed me off, and I refused to do my physical therapy and school work until they told me more. I felt like they owed me answers.

But somehow Roxanne talked me into it. She promised that once I got through the time in LA, I'd find out everything I wanted to know. So now it's time for her to pay up. I graduated from physical therapy and got my GED, and I'm even enrolled at the Smoky Falls College starting Monday. It's a little nerve-wracking to know I'll be in college classes when I haven't been inside a classroom since I was fourteen, but after the last year of hard work I should at least have enough education for a community college.

I'm desperate to find out more about my whole distant family I never heard about, not to mention my own mom and dad. All I know is that my parents left Smoky Falls when they were still young and never contacted their families again.

As we pass a painted wooden sign that read 'Welcome to Smoky Falls', an electric thrill runs through my body—this is it! The new life I've been working toward for over a year. The fresh start Roxanne promised is waiting for me. My things from the apartment we shared were packed up and shipped before we departed, and all that's left in LA now are memories.

Tomorrow is my eighteenth birthday. I check my Apple watch—another gift from Roxanne—and it's nearly seven now. In just a few short hours, I will be an adult, free to do whatever I want without the threat of foster care to keep me in line.

But I have no money, nowhere to go, and an uncle that will foot the bill for a college degree—why not take advantage? I can set myself up for whatever life I want, live here rent-free, and make my way back to LA or wherever the wind takes me once I'm done.

I peer through the windshield when I notice light up ahead; two lamp posts flank the entrance, complete with an ornate wrought-iron gate and a guardhouse. The uniformed guard steps out and verifies the driver's ID before hitting a switch that opens the gate, and our SUV rumbles quietly ahead.

Another electric wave runs through my body, setting the hairs on my arms standing at attention as we pass through the threshold. This is a heck of a lot of security—my uncle has to be *seriously* loaded. Unless this is all just the trappings of being mayor? I know Roxanne says he's rich, but she would never get into details. I wonder if he owns a fleet of fancy sports cars? A jet? A helicopter? A villa in the south of France?

We turn another corner, and there's once again light ahead. I can make out a massive stone house with warm glowing lamps decorating the castle-like exterior. As we draw closer, I spot a small group of people standing outside, waiting for our arrival.

My heart rate rises to double time. I wish once again

that Roxanne had flown with me instead of a day earlier. It would be nice to arrive with her in the car; even though I know she's waiting for me there on the steps, it feels like I am suddenly facing the unknown completely alone.

And just like that, the SUV crawls to a stop directly in front of the grand entrance. My heart absolutely pounds in my chest as I watch Roxanne step forward to open the door.

"Welcome to Smoky Falls, Layla."

Chapter Two

LAYLA

~

The lights are glaring as I step out of the dark SUV, and the air is cool and damp, just as I'd imagined it. A few people wait by the door, some of them wearing uniforms, and my eyes land on the man I can only assume is my mysterious uncle.

He isn't unattractive, although he is older than I imagined he'd be. A good deal of silver is mixed with his dark hair, and his clean-shaved face is clearly lined, even in the shadow cast by the lights behind him. Even so, he seems in better shape than most men his age. His dark eyes track my slow stumbling progress up the stairs with Roxanne by my side, and for just a second I swear I see a flash of silver reflected in their depths.

Then it's gone, and they're dark as before.

"Lilliana," the gruff voice I recognize from the phone calls rumbles. "We're so glad to have you here."

I bite back the sarcastic retorts that bubble up in my throat.

"I'd never have guessed, since you left me in LA for a year."

"Sure, even though you couldn't be bothered to come visit me once in the last year."

"It's Layla, not Lilliana."

But I'm spared having to reply, since Roxanne does it for me.

"She goes by Layla, sir."

His tone warms. "Oh, yes, I'm sorry Layla. Roxanne told me that before. Your mother... her name was Lilliana, and you look so like her, I have to remember... but no matter, I will work on it."

"What was she like when she was younger, my mom?" I'm too eager to know more about her to be couth. I've waited a year for answers, and now he's already told me things I've always wondered.

"We have plenty of time to get into that," Roxanne interjects, and eyes me meaningfully. "Why don't you show her around the house, sir?"

"Very well," my uncle answers agreeably, then fixes me with a half-smile. "Shall we?"

"Sure," I shrug. "What should I call you?"

He pauses for a moment. "You may call me Uncle, or Dominic. Or Dom. Or Uncle Dom, if you prefer. Any of those will do."

"Okay, Dom," I smile with tentative friendliness. "I'm ready when you are."

He turns around and gestures to the entrance, where an older man in a neat black suit waits to open the door. "After you."

As I approach, the man tugs on the door, bowing his head while he waits for us to pass through. I thank him, but he doesn't respond.

We stroll into a grand foyer, filled with warm light that seems to glow from everywhere. Wall sconces, lamps, and a massive chandelier hanging above us light the space, and I crane my head back to see how high the ceiling is. Easily several stories above. There's a giant set of curving stairs to the left, and a large open space directly before me that appears to have several nooks on the far side of the building. This place is much larger than I'd even imagined.

"Right over this way," Uncle Dom gestures to my right, "is the conservatory."

We step between two columns and down a few stairs, and I find myself in a round, sunken space surrounded by lush, tropical plants.

"The winters are cold here, as you'll discover soon enough. It's nice to have a little of the outside without having to leave the house. Of course, you can visit the gardens tomorrow, but for tonight we'll just do the house tour. Come along."

I follow him out the other side of the conservatory into a room dominated on one side by three giant fire-places. The ceiling is easily five stories above us, with a bank of windows on one side showing the night sky beyond. The sparkling wood floor is mostly bare, aside from one massive rectangular table with at least three dozen chairs surrounding it, all upholstered in crimson satin. Tapestries line the walls, and two giant round chandeliers fill the space with a warm glow. The sense of being in a castle grows as I stare around the cavernous space.

"This is the formal dining room. Although we don't use it very often, it is nice for special occasions," my uncle comments as we pass through.

The kitchen is just as massive, with an entire wall of modern ovens and stovetops, three refrigerators, and enough counter space to sit twenty people at a banquet.

"Uncle Dom, how old is this... house?"

"It has been in our family for generations," he replies. "Construction took nearly a decade, and they finished it in 1895. Back then, the family was... much larger. Now here," he leads me into another room, this one also featuring a table but a fraction of the size of the formal dining room. "This is where we'll have most of our meals. Roxanne will make sure you know the schedule and where to be when."

I barely have a chance to take in the dark wood-paneled walls and massive fireplace before he ushers me into the hallway and back toward the main entrance. "Now, we could take the stairs," he gestures to a giant set that spirals several stories above, "or we could take the elevator," he adds with a mischievous grin.

"Um, how far up are we going?" I ask, not sure what the right answer is.

"Let's just take the elevator for now. It's quicker." We pass the stairs into an alcove on the right, and find a small elevator with an antique gate. Uncle Dom mashes the button marked '2' and the elevator slowly climbs, rattling slightly.

"How many people live here?" It isn't very late, but I've seen a grand total of four people in this massive house.

"Right now, including you, me, and the staff... twelve. That's just the resident staff, mind. We have plenty of people who come to help with the grounds and cleaning that live in town." He continues rattling off facts about the house and I manage to take in a few details, but I'm quickly becoming overwhelmed.

The elevator finally stops and Uncle Dom opens the brass gate. "Take the first right ahead, please."

I walk forward numbly, trying to wrap my head around the number of bathrooms my uncle mentioned. Did he seriously say *forty*? How many toilets could a person possibly need?

Turning at the indicated spot, I find myself in a large, airy room featuring several massive fireplaces, multiple groupings of green velvet furniture, and floor-to-ceiling tapestries. "This is the dayroom, where you can do more casual activities."

"Casual?" I gape at him amongst the ornate furnishings and decor.

Dom chuckles. "Don't worry, it's okay to use. We

have an excellent maintenance staff. Yes, a lot of the things here are antiques, but we maintain them fairly well, and you're too old to cause too much damage from carelessness. I think we'll be okay." He gestures down the long room, and I follow, exiting the second set of double doors at the far end and crossing the hallway. "Now this room," he gestures grandly, "is our-"

"Library!" I squeal. Smaller and cozier, with an arched, hand-painted ceiling, the library boasts floor-to-ceiling shelves of books, with a balcony halfway up the two-story walls. It features another massive fireplace, and rich burgundy furnishings.

My earlier thoughts of my uncle, like the beast in his castle, weren't too far off now that I see this place. I can definitely imagine myself sprawled out on one of those couches, wasting the day reading by the fire.

Uncle Dom smiles. "A fan of books, that's right. Roxanne told me. Most of these are antiques, but you'll find a section over there with a more modern selection. Now, this way is the music room, and then we still have the games room, my office, and…"

I follow and nod along as he shows me a seemingly endless series of rooms, all featuring antique furnishings that are polished to a warm shine. I feel as though I've stepped back in time and I'm literally walking into a fairy tale. At some point I just stop being able to take any more in, but follow along and try to look engaged, anyway.

Uncle Dom shows me his office, another big-beyond-all-sense room with gleaming wood paneling, and surprisingly modern decor. At this point, my eyes just follow where he points, my vision distinctly glazed, and I hear him chuckle.

"I'm guessing that's enough for one night. Why don't I show you where your room is, and you can get settled in? Roxanne and the rest of the staff will be around to show you more tomorrow, and of course, you're welcome to explore."

I walk beside him down the hall, completely at a loss for how I'm supposed to find my way back downstairs for breakfast tomorrow. "Will you be gone?"

"I'll be around, but I always seem to have a lot of work to do, Lil- I'm sorry, Layla. So I'm afraid I'll probably be locked up in my office most of the day. I hope we can have dinner together, though. Ah, here we are."

He pushes through another set of ornate double doors, and it's as if I've walked into a completely different book than the fairy tale of a moment ago.

The beautiful wood details are still there, along with wallpaper and lush carpets. However, it's all been refreshed and modernized. The crown molding and ornate carvings are bright white, and the wallpaper is a soft lilac covered in a rich, raised pattern with metallic accents. I've found myself in a cozy sitting room, complete with its own enormous fireplace, a large flat screen mounted above, and a small dining area.

I stare back at my uncle in wonder, and he just grins. "Roxanne had it redone, hopefully to your taste. Your bedroom is through there," he points to another set of double doors, and I run to throw them open. I'm giddy with excitement now, and the room beyond does not disappoint.

A king-sized, four-poster bed waits for me, modern and draped with gauzy curtains, the mattress topped with a fluffy white comforter and entirely too many pillows in shades of purple and white. The room has high domed ceilings with a 'cherubs in heaven motif', and thick carpets on the gleaming wooden floor. Yet another fireplace, and two more doors.

The first door leads to a gorgeous modern bathroom with dual sinks, a sparkling white vanity that seems to go on forever, a large steam shower, and a deep stand-alone tub. Everything screams new, but fits elegantly in with the antique style of the house.

Uncle Dom grins widely from his spot leaning against the doorframe, watching me explore with child-like enthusiasm. "Wait till you see the closet," he hints, pointing at the second door I had yet to open.

Wasting no time, I throw it open to find a dressing room fit for a queen with a snowy white interior. Racks and shelves line the wall, a bank of drawers on each side, and a large white velvet bench in the middle. All of my possessions from LA already hang neatly on the racks or are tucked into drawers, my shoes displayed on shelves as if they are priceless pieces of art. Besides my existing wardrobe, it's obvious there are easily three times more things than I've ever owned waiting for me. Likely all chosen by Roxanne, and likely all beautiful and perfectly fit.

It's too much. Far too much for me to handle.

Emotion wells in my throat and the tears pour from my eyes out of nowhere.

"Erm, that is not the reaction I was expecting." Uncle Dom clears his throat awkwardly. "If you don't like it, I'm sure we can re-do it all. It's not a problem. Roxanne-"

"No," I sniff and try to smile in his direction. "It's beautiful, really, and I'm so grateful. It's just so much, I don't know. I think I'm just overwhelmed."

"Ah, well, in that case, perhaps you'd like a little time to get settled? All your things are already here, but if you have trouble finding anything, just text Roxanne. She can tell you where to find your stuff. I have a meeting tonight, but they'll be bringing dinner up for you shortly. We figured we'd keep it low key tonight and... just let you have your space."

"Thank you," I say again, following him back out through my private living room. "I'm really looking forward to exploring the house and grounds. I'm probably just a little tired."

"Er, yes, about that," he turns suddenly on his heels and fixes me with a stern expression. "You have free access to anywhere in the house, with the exception of my room and office, if I'm not in there. I'm sure you can respect my privacy and I will not enter your room without your permission, either. Mutual respect?" He raises one eyebrow.

I nod. "Of course, Uncle Dom."

"Good," he smiles warmly. "One other thing: You

are welcome to explore the grounds, but do not go out after dark, especially in the areas near the forest."

"Why?"

"This isn't LA, kid. This is Appalachia. The woods are filled with wild animals, like bears, and they're not cute or cuddly. Do you understand?"

"I understand."

"Good," he says again. "Tomorrow, if you'd like to explore, Roxanne can set you up with one of the ground staff, or you can explore on your own. Just stay out of the forest if you're alone. Deal?"

"Deal." I grin, excited at the prospect of adventuring.

"Goodnight, Layla. I'm very glad you're here, and I hope it feels like home to you soon. I know it's a lot, but... it's your birthright."

Anxiety wells in my chest. "Uncle Dom, I have so many questions about my mom and this place. When-"

"Let's talk tomorrow at dinner, okay? For tonight, you just focus on getting settled and getting some rest. Oh, and the tv has any streaming service you could want. If you need help, just text Roxanne. Her room's not far. Goodnight, Layla."

With another warm smile, he shows himself out of my suite, and I am again alone.

Milo

I feel it as soon as she enters the pack territory. An electric sensation runs over my skin, sending shivers through my body and raising my heart rate. I set down my phone for fear the electricity in my blood will short circuit the device and focus on breathing steadily.

Dad always said he felt it the day Mom was born. At first it was like a low buzz in the back of his mind, easy to tune out. Then his skin became alive the day of her birth on pack lands, forming the instant, unbreakable bond of a fated pair.

He was several years older than her, so he recalls clearly. Others just grow up with their mate and don't know any different. The Pack Seer predicts the mate pairings at birth and tracks every one.

Landon, Jared and I were all born within hours of each other, and all fated to mate the next Harridan alpha.

Which threw the world into absolute chaos.

Because the last Harridan alpha disappeared before completing the manifestation, which left Dominic Harridan no choice but to assume the role. According to the pack historians, there has never been an unmated male alpha. Period. Dominic was never assigned a fated mate at birth, and typically in those cases they are welcome to search the other packs for another unmated, or live among the humans and marry one of them.

Meanwhile, the status as alpha is typically passed from mother to daughter, and the born alpha always

17

has three mates to share the responsibility. That's the way it's always been: four alphas in Smoky Falls.

Of course, I only know that from lessons. Since I can remember, there has only been Dom Harridan. Lilliana Harridan fled with one of her mates, leaving the other two behind. They didn't know where she'd gone, and they never got over it.

But that buzzing my father described was a message to Landon, Jared and I. Because we felt it, the same sensation, telling us our mate was out there but not within the pack boundary. We had endless discussions about how long we should wait to see if she comes back, if she knows about us or her own history. About when we should decide we were officially rejected and seek another life besides the one we were born to live.

Now, just like that, the world has tilted on its axis. Dom said that would happen back when he warned us he'd found her and was bringing her back to Smoky Falls. We'd been waiting nearly a year to meet our mate, the born alpha of the Smoky Falls pack. Dominic also warned us she did not know her wolf heritage, and that we'd have to keep it under wraps until the time was right.

There was no question of disobeying him; an order from the alpha is not something you can ignore. Even a stand-in like Dom, with no mates at all, has the basic compulsion powers of an alpha. Once mated, of course, that power multiplies and unifies the pack. And soon it would be our job to help the new alpha claim her birthright.

My phone buzzes, startling me from my thoughts.

I don't need to look at the screen to know who it is.

"Hey Landon."

"Did you feel it?" His voice is practically shaking with excitement.

"Yeah, I felt it."

"It's just like my pa said!"

"Yep," I agree.

"Where do you think she is right now?"

"Probably at the manor, or on her way if she's not there yet."

"Do you think we'll see her tonight?"

"No. She doesn't know about the wolves yet, remember?"

"Oh, yeah, right." His disappointment is palpable. "When do you think we'll get to meet her?"

"I have an idea about that."

"I'm all ears!"

"How do you feel about landscaping?"

"I like to be outside."

"Yeah, I know. What I mean is, how do you feel about helping? With landscaping. At the manor?"

"Oooooh, I got you. Yeah, that's a great idea. I'm in!"

"Okay. We'll have to play it cool and just... see if we cross her path. No promises, but at least we can go with my dad tomorrow and have the excuse to see her before classes start Monday. If nothing else, Dom said we'll see her there. All her classes are with at least one of us so she's never alone."

"Oh, yeah, that's probably smart."

"No shit, given everyone that'll be there."

"Do you think they'll be a problem?"

"Do you doubt it?"

Landon sighs heavily. "I hope they won't, but something tells me it's a vain hope."

"Yeah, me too. Well, she has us, even if she doesn't know it yet."

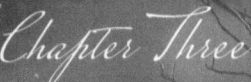

Chapter Three

LAYLA

~

My eyes snap open, my heart racing. I'm nestled in my giant bed, surrounded by pillows, and soaked with sweat.

What woke me?

It's dark. I have no idea what time, but it doesn't feel close to morning. Groggily, I reach for my phone on the nightstand and check. It's quarter after midnight.

The house is quiet, aside from the low hum of the heat running. I lay for a few minutes, trying to sort out why I'm awake. I feel as if something startled me out of sleep, but I don't know what.

Then, in the distance, I hear it: The howling of wolves. It starts out as a single wolf releasing a sharp, lamenting keen, and then more join in until it's a chorus of wolf calls. A shiver runs down my spine.

Suddenly, the dream I'd interrupted by waking comes back to me.

In the dream, I was a wolf. I was running through the forest with my pack, leading them, charging along the wooded path under bright moonlight.

Well, that makes sense. Hear wolf calls, dream about wolves.

Now that I'm awake, hunger gnaws a hole in my belly. I didn't eat much dinner because it felt too early for the meal, and since the household staff removed the dinner tray, I was paying the price. While I was excited about this massive house and my personal suite of rooms at first, I now recognize the downfall.

Because all that house lay between me and a snack.

I try to go back to sleep for a while until I realize it's no use. The hunger pang in my stomach grows more insistent, and I finally throw the covers back and stand.

Roxanne gave me a quick tour of my rooms before bed, so I knew where to find a thick fluffy robe and slippers. Using the flashlight on my phone, I exit my room and make my way down the hall toward the elevator.

It takes me a minute to realize I'm being excessively quiet, as though I'm attempting to be sneaky. My heart is racing and palms sweating, like I'm doing something wrong.

But this isn't the foster house. There's no lock on the fridge, and no one is going to beat me with a belt for being out of bed. At our apartment in LA, Roxanne let me eat whenever and whatever I wanted, provided I had three reasonable meals a day. She never forbade snacks or treats, which at first was too much for me to handle.

I hoarded stuff in my room for months, fearful that it would be taken away or I'd have to grab my stuff and run. Gradually I started putting it back in the cupboard, and if she noticed, she never said a word. By the end of our year, I had complete faith that no matter when I wanted it, food would be there for me to have. I got used to snacking, and lately it seems like I am always hungry.

After four years of foster care and street life, Roxanne tamed the feral beast I'd become into a reasonable approximation of a domesticated teenager. Even so, I make a mental note to ask her to put a small fridge and snack cupboard in my closet. There's plenty of space, and then if I'm up late, I don't need to traverse the Appalachian Trail to get a snack.

I take the little elevator downstairs, the light from my phone all the illumination I have. Once out on the ground floor, the giant windows let in a decent amount of moonlight, and I have no problem finding my way to the kitchen.

I locate some cheese, bottled water, and crackers without turning on any lights. For some reason, it feels as though flipping a switch would trip an alarm that sends staff scurrying to find me, and I definitely don't want to wake them. Although now that I think about it, the house feels empty. Of course it's massive beyond all sense, and only twelve people live here. But even early this evening, I could feel the presence of other people. Right now, I feel like the only soul alive in this place.

The wolves continue their howling outside, sending another sudden shiver racing up my spine. I shove my pockets full of snacks, then head back the way I came and up the elevator. The second story hallway is deathly quiet, and I listen for any telltale signs of other humans like snoring or creaking floorboards, but none reach my ears before I close my suite door.

Once I've finished my snack and my tummy is happy, I slide back under the covers and lay back on my nest of pillows.

The wolf howls are far in the distance now, almost inaudible, and I drift off peacefully.

❧

Layla

❧

"Good morning, Layla!" A soft knock on my door startles me awake, and Roxanne steps in, beaming. "Happy birthday!" She's already caffeinated and dressed for the day, her neat black braids woven into a thick plait down her back.

"Thank you," I answer groggily, sitting up. "What time is it?"

"Just after nine. I've had the housekeeper bring up

your breakfast so they can clean up the kitchen. Everything here runs on a schedule, but you'll adapt quickly. Your uncle really wanted you to have the opportunity to explore and settle in, so we don't have much of an agenda for the weekend."

"Wait, what are you going to do?" I sound like a whiny child, but I can't help it. The bizarre fear that she was suddenly going to disappear for good sent anxiety racing through my chest.

"I work for your uncle, so I'll be in his office most of the day, I'm sure. It's been a while since I was here to organize and I have a feeling there's a sea of chaos waiting for me." She chuckles. "But I won't be far, okay? If you need something, just text me." She checks the phone in her hand as if to demonstrate how easy she is to reach.

"Oh, okay." My earlier excitement for exploring sours. Somehow, the realization that I will be alone all day drains the fun from the plan.

When did that happen? Before we left LA, all I wanted was to be alone. And now the idea is indescribably depressing.

My face must reflect my disappointment, because Roxanne leaves the doorway and sits on my bed. Her phone buzzes on the comforter, but she leaves it face down. "Hey, I know it's a lot of change and you're probably home sick. But it'll get better, I promise. And this weekend is just for you to get settled in. Starting Monday, you'll have classes and friends and activities, and you'll probably start begging for alone time."

"I don't know why everyone keeps saying I need to 'settle in,'" I grumble. "All of my stuff was already put away when I got here. There's literally nothing for me to settle."

"Just your spirit, Layla. It's a chance for you to take ownership of the space and make it feel like your own."

"Speaking of ownership of the space..." I tell her about my fridge and snacks cupboard idea, and she assures me she'll take care of it.

"Now, your breakfast is growing cold, so why don't you go eat and enjoy your day? We'll have a nice dinner tonight for your birthday." With a warm hug, Roxanne stands and bustles from the room. She's already got the phone raised to her ear before she's out of my suite.

I flick the tv on to watch a show about a fairy academy while I eat and try not to be lonely.

Chapter Four

LAYLA

~

Morning in the Smoky Mountains is misty and cool, but after a self-pep talk I'm again eager to get outside and explore. I tuck my phone into my jeans pocket and pull on a fuzzy cream-colored sweater, then take the elevator down and dart for the door. I'm a little afraid Roxanne will insist on sending a chaperone with me, so my mission is to get out unseen.

Once I descend the stone steps, I'm not sure where to go. In the foggy daylight, I can definitely see more of the property than I could last night, but it seems to disappear a hundred yards away. Uncle Dom said the property is six thousand acres... that's definitely big enough for me to get completely lost in, and I suddenly second-guess my desire to wander alone.

But my stubborn side kicks in. After a year under close supervision, I'm itching for the freedom this place offers. After all, I spent years on the streets taking care of myself. Derrek was there, and the other kids, but we all knew we were really on our own. Besides, it's not like I'm a complete moron. Roxanne clearly feels more relaxed about my safety here, so as long as I don't go into the woods, I should be able to find myself back to the house just fine.

House, I snort to myself. Castle, more like. *I shouldn't have a problem finding my way back to the castle.*

Tucking my fingers into the soft weave of my sweater, I turn right and start marching into the mist. It's quiet, the blanket of fog suppressing any sound aside from the crunch of gravel under my feet. The further I go, the more I can see in the distance. First a row of very tall trees, like ghostly sentries, rise from the mist. They appear to line the long oval driveway. Beyond them is a wall made of the same tan stone as the main building, and then a set of descending stairs lies directly in front of me, with a large, empty court-yard on my level to the right like an extension of the house.

Once down the stairs, I spot another narrow courtyard on the left, except this one isn't empty. It's filled with a series of large ponds, and high walls on either side support trellises of vines that shade benches every twenty feet. I can't see how far back it goes in the fog, and the sense of the world dropping off just out of sight raises the hairs on my arms. I continue quickly, heading straight and finding myself on a long stone walkway butted up against a high wall to the right, covered by a series of arbors thick with vines. A large fountain is mounted to the wall, featuring a dancing fish spraying water, and a set of stairs to the left with a small sign that reads 'Green House.'

My heart beats quickly as I descend yet another set of steps. It's not like it's a lot of exercise, but there's something exhilarating about wandering around this misty garden alone. It's like at any time a person—or a beast—could materialize out of the fog. But I have yet to run into another soul, even though I'm sure they're out there. *Somewhere.*

I follow a winding trail, this one paved, through a more natural section of the garden. There are ghostly trees at a distance of a couple hundred yards on both sides, but the area around the path seems rather well-manicured. All the plants are cultivated, with small signs in the mulch explaining their species. A narrow path of wood chips veers off the main trail, circling one of the larger beds up over a hill, and I decide to follow it. It's a path. Surely it's safe enough.

I didn't realize how damp the ground was until now. The woodchips sink into the soft earth beneath my feet and the grass around the path appears almost muddy.

And that's when I see them: clear, distinct canine prints in the mud. And they're large, almost as big as my own feet. They seem to exit the forest and end on the trail, as if the wolf enjoyed a casual stroll through the gardens last night.

Well, now my uncle's warning to stay out of the woods because of animals definitely hits home. I can't imagine the size of the monster that made those prints. It had to be up to my chest! I've never heard of a wolf that large.

I whip out my phone to research wolves in the Smoky Mountains, but I have no signal. *Figures*.

Tucking the device back in my pocket, I continue on the trail and ignore the shiver that runs down my spine.

You're not in LA anymore, Layla.

Before long, the woodchips lead me back to the main paved trail, and I continue a gradual descent until I reach yet another set of steps. An ornate wooden arbor guards this one, and when I reach the bottom I'm looking out over even *more* gardens.

The area is clear, massive, and neatly cultivated. At least as large as a football field, it's ringed with neat rows of plants as far as the eye can see. The mist clings to everything, so I can't make out too much detail. However, I see a long vine-covered arbor creating a center path, with curving walkways weaving to the left and the right among hundreds of rose bushes. Far in the distance, barely visible in the thick fog, are the peaks of several massive glass buildings.

My excitement grows, and I head straight down the central path. I can enjoy the roses on a sunny day, but in my life I'd never imagined such a large greenhouse. When I saw the sign, I pictured a tiny little hut made of glass with a central aisle and a single row on either side to support a few plants.

As I get closer, I can really appreciate the size. There are four altogether, each with their own set of double doors, and easily three stories tall. In the distance, I hear the hum of a vehicle, but I still have yet to see a living soul. I can see the tops of palm trees—*palm trees!*—in the peaked roofs of glass, so I head for the second building and tug on one of the heavy wooden doors.

It opens far more easily than I expect, and I feel as if I'm Dorothy, suddenly going from black and white Kansas to the bright garish colors of Oz. There is a riot of color in here, and it's absolutely astonishing. Every shade of green imaginable bursts from the beds, with colorful tropical flowers dispersed among the lush greenery. Plants tower overhead and pour down the walls, vines crawling across every surface. Immediately inside the door is a path to the left or right, wrapping around a large central bed and connecting to the greenhouse on either side. The air is balmy and, although damp, its dryer than the mountain mist.

I decide to wander right, taking in the bright colors as the warm tropical air chases the chill from my skin. When I reach the doors to the next greenhouse, I pass through to find myself in an orchid oasis. Not only are there tumbling waterfalls of large white blossoms, but stems bearing every shape and color of the flower surround me on all sides like colorful ribbons. They grafted orchids onto palm trees, their spindly roots sticking out at all angles to draw moisture from the air.

Potted orchids are tucked into nests of greenery in another large central planter. It's so much. I feel that pressure in my chest again, the overwhelm that I grappled with last night.

Orchids were mom's favorite flower, but she could never get them to re-bloom in our series of dark little apartments. I remember she'd be so happy when dad brought her one as a surprise, but as the blooms wilted she'd grow sad, and eventually frustrated that they never flowered again.

Being here, surrounded by hundreds of gorgeous, blooming orchids, I can finally understand what she was missing. This was her *home*. I want to believe she left for a reason, but I can't help but wonder what it could be. Why on earth did she run away and leave all of this behind? No one in their right mind could possibly see the sense in it.

Sighing, I reach a tentative hand out to stroke a snowy-white blossom. The petal is like velvet between my fingers, unbelievably delicate. I smile to myself, remembering how mom always did the same thing.

"You'd better not let Larry catch you doing that," a soft male voice startles me, and I pull my hand back as if the flower had burned me. "Pretty sure he considers those things his babies."

I whirl around to find the source of the voice, and spot a ridiculously hot guy leaning casually against the door frame I'd just passed through. The first thing I notice are piercing blue eyes that seem to be lit with an internal source, sparkling in amusement. He's at least half a foot taller than me, nearly six feet, with dark hair cut long on top and artfully coiffed in a stylish disarray. A light dusting of stubble graces his angled jaw, accentuating full lips that are curved in a casual, one-sided smile. He's wearing jeans with a green button-down shirt and the sleeves rolled up, revealing strong, pale forearms. Clearly muscular, but not big like a football player.

It rattles my nerves. "Don't you know better than to sneak up on people?" I snap, trying not to appear too interested. A pulse of adrenaline burst in my body the second my eyes landed on him. I wasn't expecting a sexy guy around my age to be the first person I bumped into on my uncle's property. Particularly in the greenhouse, I was expecting more old and wrinkly.

"My apologies, princess," he smirks. "I thought I made plenty of noise, but you seemed to be lost in your thoughts."

I bristle at being called 'princess.' On the street, a nickname like that meant you couldn't hack it, and it still makes my blood boil. "And who are *you*, exactly?"

He steps forward, wearing a friendly grin with his hand extended. "Milo Vernice, pleasure to meet you. And you are?"

I narrow my eyes at his hand, refusing to take it. "Layla... well, I guess technically my name is Lilliana Harridan. I don't know if I'll get used to that one, but it's apparently what my birth certificate says."

"But you prefer Layla?" His hand still doesn't drop, like it's some kind of battle of wills.

I fold my arms across my chest. "Well, actually I prefer Lex. It's what I went by on... back home. But Layla is what my parents called me."

"That's a lot of names for one girl. I can understand why you're confused." He smirks, and it's incredibly irritating that he's even hotter when he's mocking me.

"Wait, I'm not-"

"But if you prefer Lex, then that is what I'll call you," he finishes with a grin. "Nice to meet you, Lex." He moves his hand forward slightly, his grin widening.

I sigh and slip mine into his, accepting the handshake. His fingers are warm and smooth, and when we touch it almost feels like an electric current passes between our bodies.

Milo's voice is rich and smooth, like a natural singer. "Welcome to Smoky Falls, Lex."

I take a minute to realize I've frozen, gripping his hand and staring into his dark eyes like a crazy person. I jump back and shove my hands into my pockets.

"Thanks." I rack my brain for something else to say. "So, do you work here?"

"Nah, I just came up today to help my dad. He's one of the groundskeepers, and there's always a lot to do."

For someone doing manual outdoor labor, he seems pretty clean. But I choose to keep that observation to myself.

"Seems like an easy way to make some extra money." I look around, wondering if I could get in on that and maybe learn how to care for orchids. Especially since he doesn't seem to be doing much. I had yet to be offered cash of any kind, despite all the extravagant gifts Roxanne and my uncle have given me.

Milo chuckles. "I don't get paid. I'm just helping out."

"Well, that's awfully generous of you. Do you help in here with the orchids?"

"Nope, like I said, those are Larry's babies. I just came in here to look for-"

Right then, a loud crash from the door opening sounds in the next greenhouse over.

"My friend," Milo snorts. He raises his voice to shout, "Hey Landon, over here!"

I turn to take in the newcomer as he approaches, and I feel the same visceral pulse through my body as soon as my gaze lands on him. My cheeks warm with embarrassment. For some reason, my physical reaction to these boys is super dramatic, and I sure as hell don't want them to know.

The second guy is even taller, at least a foot taller than my 5'3" and slightly thinner with blonde-highlighted hair. He's got a cleft chin and soulful eyes with sharp, straight brows and high cheekbones. Combined with a beauty mark just above his left dimple and the dark jeans slung low on his hips, the dude looks like he should headline a band somewhere.

I'd go see him, even if he sucked. That kind of eye candy is worth the assault on the ears.

Landon's eyes land on mine and he beelines straight for me with surprising intensity.

Milo's voice sounds amused. "Landon, meet Layla. Or Lex. Or Lilliana."

Landon quirks a brow. "All of 'em, huh?"

A nervous laugh escapes my lips. "Layla is fine."

His full lips curve into an irresistible smile, and he presents his hand for a shake. "Then it's my pleasure, Layla." When I accept his shake, another spark passes between us, and he raises my hand to press a kiss to the back.

It takes everything I have not to melt into a puddle right there.

When Landon releases my hand with a wink, I tuck it safely in my pocket and turn awkwardly back to Milo. "So, you're both here 'helping out'?" I glance between the two of them, not really sure where to look. They're flanking me and the heat from their bodies invades my space.

It's not entirely an unpleasant sensation, but I'm so programmed to keep my distance for my own safety that I'm fighting the urge to scoot.

"Yeah, but we're pretty much done. What are you up to?" Milo's eyes are warm, and something I see in them calms me slightly.

"I'm exploring." I shrug. "I just arrived from LA last night, and this is my first time out of California. So it's a lot to take in. I've never seen anything like it."

Milo exchanges a glance with Landon over my head before he returns his gaze to mine. "Would you like a tour?"

Chapter Five

LANDON

~

I know it's shitty, but some part of me is incredibly relieved that Layla is hot. I mean, she's going to be my mate for the rest of my life, so I think it's fair to be happy that I'm attracted to her.

She's got this wild dark hair that my fingers are itching to touch and see if it's as soft as it looks, and bright green eyes that practically glow in the low light of day. She said she moved here from LA, but her skin is pale and creamy, and even though she's tiny compared to me, her body is deliciously curvy. And she's got this look to her that's like, innocent but wise beyond her years.

Milo's dad told us everything he knew on the drive over. Basically, her parents died, and they put her in foster care because no one knew of their connection to Smoky Falls. She had a shitty foster home and ran away, then lived on the streets for a few years before she was attacked and Dom saw her on the news.

What a crazy story. What were the odds that we would have ever found her, if not for that attack?

But as we wander around the grounds, talking about Smoky Falls and introducing her to her new home, she doesn't seem out of sorts. In fact, she seems to have adapted really well already. She's chatty and curious about the town, the school, and what people do for entertainment.

Milo and I are careful to avoid discussing wolves in any way, and just present ourselves as friends and future classmates. Soon enough Dom will explain everything about the pack to her, but he gave strict orders that no one was to speak to her about wolves, and the weight of the alpha's command keeps the word off our tongues.

That is until she brings it up.

"Hey, let me show you guys something. Maybe you can answer a question for me."

"Sure thing, Lex." Milo is always effortlessly cool, but even in the face of our long-lost mate, he seems completely unruffled. I felt the change when she came through the pack barriers last night, but now it feels like constant energy zipping over my skin. Just being close to her, getting whiffs of her sweet cherry-almond scent, is doing crazy things to my body. The alpha command certainly helps, but it is also taking a lot of willpower to stop myself from pressing my body to hers and burying my nose in her hair. My every instinct is pushing me to touch her as much as I can, and I keep my hands in my pockets to avoid freaking her out.

Milo seems completely unaffected. Ass.

Layla leads us off the paved path along a trail, and points at the ground. "Are those wolf's prints? I mean, they look like wolf prints, but I've never seen any in person, and I didn't know they would be so big. My uncle didn't tell me anything about wolves around here."

Milo crouches down and pretends to examine the prints. Any idiot can tell they're wolf prints. There's certainly no need for such a thorough examination.

"To be honest, I'm not really sure," he answers carefully and stands. "What did your uncle say?"

"Well I haven't asked him yet. I just saw them on my walk down to the greenhouse," she rolls her eyes as if this should be obvious. Which, of course, it is, but Milo's playing dumb. "But last night he told me to stay out of the woods because of bears, and he never mentioned wolves."

"Oh, yeah, the bears can be dangerous, especially around this time of year," I latch onto the subject, the stress of the alpha command straining my throat as I skirt the wolf subject. "They're preparing to hibernate, so they get especially mean as food gets scarce. Particularly the mommas with their cubs."

"Yeah, best to stay away from the bears," Milo agrees. "Shall we?" He gestures down the path toward the alpha house, deliberately stepping on the prints in the mud to ruin them.

"Wait, but-"

"You know, I think I could go for some hot chocolate. Susan, the sous chef in the house, makes the most amazing hot chocolate. Should we go bribe her to make some?" Milo wags his eyebrows, and somehow he even manages to make hot cocoa sound cool.

"You want hot cocoa?" Layla looks confused. "It's not even that cold out."

"Yeah, but the dampness in the air is chilly," I add, "and her cocoa is really tough to beat. No offense, but I'm pretty sure Milo is just using our new acquaintance with you just to get cocoa. Which, to be honest, I don't blame him for. It's *that* good."

Layla snorts a laugh. "Well, alright then, I guess we can go get some cocoa. Doesn't seem like I'll see much more of the grounds until the fog lifts, anyway."

∽

Layla

∽

Spending the afternoon with Milo and Landon is... nice. Even though they're both really cute and I'm not used to having nice boys, obviously from good families, look at me that way. There's something about them that feels like home. It's tough to put my finger on, precisely.

There's a sense of safety around them. The tingling sensation happens whenever we make contact; although it doesn't happen often, it sends a thrill through me each time.

We enjoy our cocoa—Milo wasn't kidding, it's the best I've ever had, made with real melted chocolate— and he flirts with the older woman until she forks over some cookies in a secret stash I didn't know about. Then she shoos us out of the kitchen so she can get started on dinner.

How weird is it they know more about my home than I do?

Milo admits his father has worked here since before he was born, so he's practically grown up on the grounds. Something tells me that knowledge might be useful to me later.

After they leave, I return to my room and mull over why these two guys that I just met feel so exciting and yet so familiar. It takes me a long time to puzzle the connection out.

And I finally conclude that something about them— something nebulous and difficult to grasp—reminds me of Derrek, and that's why.

My heart still squeezes whenever I think about Derrek. Yes, he's a much older guy who treated me with all the interest of a kid sister, but I can admit I had quite the crush on him. He was bigger, smarter, fiercely protective, and I pretty much worshipped the ground he walked on.

He seemed to be respected by most of the people

who might cause a group of street kids trouble. Local gang leaders would visit, even the pimps, and on occasion, even street cops.

I'd learned how to pilfer small things at the foster home—when the fridge and pantry are always padlocked, you figure out how to get food or you starve. Derrek taught me how to pick the right target, the one who would always have a wad of cash: a shiny, nondescript vehicle. Expensive-looking suit, flashy watch. I learned quick, and I survived.

Street life wasn't easy, but Derrek at least made sure we never fell victim to predators or drugs. His one rule was no drugs and no tricks. Petty theft was our bracket, and we stayed in that boundary. Anyone who stepped outside the line was no longer in Derrek's protection and had to leave immediately.

We never saw them again.

Derrek found me barely a day after I ran away from the foster house. I was with him for almost three years before the attack. I trusted him implicitly, and he always looked out for me.

Which is why it hurt that he never visited me in the hospital.

I called the hospital they originally took me to, where I stayed for three days before Uncle Dom moved me to Mount Sinai. I don't remember it, I was in a medically induced coma the entire time. Providence St. Joseph was not an exclusive place, and the ambulance would have told him where they were taking me—he's the one who called them, after all—so he knew where I was for those three days at least. But the head nurse assured me I had no visitors for the first two days I was there, until my uncle showed up with an army of attorneys and his own doctor in tow.

During my time in the apartment with Roxanne, she forbade me from returning to North Hollywood, and the need to obey her was strong. I didn't want to end up on the street again, now that I had a chance at a good life.

So I never went back.

I'm deep in my thoughts, curled up on the couch, when Roxanne knocks softly at the door and comes in beaming.

"Happy birthday again, Layla! Has the heavy mantle of adulthood settled on your shoulders?"

"Ha, not exactly," I snort. "I don't think it's quite sunken in yet." In fact, I've completely forgotten about it. Street life doesn't prepare you for people making a big deal of your birthday. More often than not, you just try to pretend it's just another day, so it doesn't hurt to think about. You try not to dwell on the memories of days when someone cared, and surprised you with gifts and balloons. You try not to remember.

But Derrek always remembered, a soft voice whispers in the back of my head.

"Well, all things in due time," Roxanne says. "Do you want to change before dinner?"

I glance down at my jeans and sweater combo. Everything is clean and neat enough. My parents were never ones to get fancy, and then I was living on the street. Even a year later I'm not used to having endless options for wardrobe, but Roxanne has tried to impress on me the variations of clothes for different formalities of occasions. "Is this not appropriate for dinner tonight?" I ask tentatively.

Roxanne beams, and my chest warms in response to her approval.

"Well, since it's your first 'real' dinner here *and* your birthday, I think your uncle has something slightly more formal in mind. Perhaps a dress? There's a row of cocktail dresses on the left side of your closet in the back. Any of them would work."

"Okay," I agree, rising from the nest of blankets I made on my couch.

"Are you cold in here?" She asks suddenly, observing the way I was bundled. "The thermostat is by the door, and we can always send someone up to start a fire for you if you like."

"Oh, no I'm fine. I was just being cozy." No need to tell her that being swathed in layers of blankets makes me feel safe—with no proper shelter on the street, I just wrapped myself up in as many blankets as I could. I haven't done it for a while, but clearly the change of scenery is making me feel a little out of sorts.

"Alright. Well, how about you meet us in the break-fast room in half an hour for dinner? Is that enough time to get ready?"

I shrug. "Sure, sounds good." I was just planning on pulling down any dress and slipping it on, which should take me about thirty seconds. Suddenly the realization hits that I'm expected to 'get ready', which is a lot more involved.

"Great, I'll see you downstairs!" Roxanne closes the door gently and bustles off.

Sighing, I drag my hands over my face and pass through my bedroom, heading into the massive closet. True to her instruction, there's an entire rack of dresses, varying from light, casual sundresses to long-sleeved cotton, and finishing with several knee-length short-sleeved dresses in various colors.

Running my fingers over them all, I pause on the small selection of warm-looking cotton dresses. It's not the season for them yet, but they're incredibly soft to the touch and I suddenly find myself looking forward to wearing them.

Which, is weird. I've never cared about clothes before. My mind drifts to Milo and Landon, and heat creeps up my cheeks again. I was imagining how they'd react to seeing me in the dresses, and that was the source of my sudden interest.

Oh man, am I suddenly reaching the 'boy crazy' stage my mom always teased me about? She insisted it'd happen in high school, but since I sort of skipped that part, it hadn't happened. I had more important things to think about, like food and shelter and safety. No time for boys, crush on Derrek not withstanding.

Shaking myself out of the tainted memories, I return to the task at hand. After selecting a dark purple dress with crystal beading, I locate a matching pair of ornate low heels. Formality might require me to don pantyhose, but that simply will *not* happen. Roxanne can be disappointed with me all she wants. I hate pantyhose.

Once I'm appropriately dressed, I head into the bathroom where all the beauty supplies Roxanne purchased for me are neatly arranged and waiting for my use. After a year of her tutelage, I'm at least decent with makeup, so I use a minimal amount of complexion products, just a little powder and blush, and focus on my eyes. The purple pallette makes it easy to coordinate with my dress and brings out the green eyes I inherited from my mom. I ignore the squeeze in my heart that always comes when I think of her, willing myself not to tear up. It might be understandable, maybe even appropriate, to shed a tear or two on my eighteenth birthday for my parents and everything I've been through, but I clench my jaw and refuse. A little liner and mascara, then gloss on my lips and I'm done.

I drag a brush through a few sections of my hair, but to be honest, I have no interest in trying to style my mane. It's wild and curly, and I kind of like the way it looks just naturally. As a nod to what Roxanne taught me, I clip one side back with a decorative barrette, then call it good.

Checking my watch, I can tell I'm a little early, but better early than late—another pro tip from Roxanne. I head downstairs and find my way to the breakfast room easily enough. The nooks in the main living space that were too dark to see last night are interesting little arrangements of furniture with distinct purposes. One a music room with a small piano and two chairs facing it.

Another some kind of formal sitting area for four. Yet another is a small reading area, with a low shelf of books and a pair of cozy chairs, a fuzzy throw blanket draped invitingly over each.

Even though I'm early, when I walk through the doors, I'm clearly the last to arrive. The adults are all standing around sipping champagne. They rush to welcome me, Roxanne giving me a warm hug and Uncle Dom an awkward pat on the back. Even Dr. Rosen is here, and the household staff who aren't serving dinner join us at the table as well. Roxanne hands me a glass of champagne with a wink, and whispers, 'happy birthday', yet again.

Of course there's a stack of presents, plenty of things I don't need and a pile of books from my wish list. They delight in watching me open the gifts, and I try not to be too awkward about it all.

It's a struggle to rein in my emotions, the tears stinging my eyes that I refuse to let fall. Not only is it overwhelming, but the last time I had a birthday party —which this definitely feels like a party, despite the lack of decorations—was the year before my parents died. It was smaller, with just a couple of friends, but that was the pinnacle of happiness in my life until now.

Am I happier now? It's difficult to say. I'm an adult, although I can't fool myself with the belief that the title carries any sort of independence. I have regained a future I thought was lost to me forever, and in fact, a life I never knew I was destined for. Every girl grows up dreaming that she's secretly a princess, and this definitely feels like I've actually drawn that winning lottery number.

On the surface, everything is wonderful. The people are kind and generous. I'm being pampered and adored in the way every lonely street kid can only dream about. I think about my street family and a pang of sadness washes through me, wishing I could share my good fortune with them and feeling just a little guilty for being here.

Despite the festive atmosphere, something is telling me this party isn't just about me. So many smiling faces, drinking to my good health and celebrating my safe return from obscurity, but the warning blaring from my inner voice is difficult to ignore. My return means something to them other than a long-lost niece returned. I can't say how, but I know it.

And I can't forget that my parents ran away from this place. I remember my parents vividly: they were smart, careful, and alert. They constantly chided me about keeping secrets, and I knew, even at a young age, that we were hiding. I just didn't know from what.

So despite how wonderful it seems, there has to be more to this story.

When I finally settle into my bed, alone at last, I promise myself that I'm going to search for the truth tomorrow. My mother grew up in this house, so it seems as good a place as any to unravel the mystery.

When someone gives you something, there's always more than meets the eye, as Derrek says. And I'm determined to find out what it is they don't want me to see.

Chapter Six

LAYLA

~

The next morning it's pouring outside. It would be nice to sleep in, but I'm determined to get up early. Despite being awakened in the middle of the night by another wolf dream, I make a point to be downstairs for breakfast. I need to show face, observe how things work, and try to get a feel for which of the household staff might have known my mom. Uncle Dom hasn't offered any more information about her, but then again, I haven't asked. However, there are lots of people bustling around the house that seem old enough to have been here twenty years ago.

My secondary goal is to make sure no one is suspicious about what I'm up to. I know Uncle Dom said he welcomes questions about my mom, and Roxanne promised I'd get all the answers I could ask for when we arrived, but so far no one has been very forthcoming. So, I'm going to see what I can learn just by poking around before I come at them with direct questions.

My mouth waters before I even reach the breakfast room, and I breathe in the aromas of fresh-baked bread, bacon, pancakes and coffee. Breakfast is incredible, with an excessive spread to choose from laid out on the banquet table. Uncle Dom already has a full plate when I arrive, and the household staff are selecting their food. Anyone who was reaching for something when I walk in the door backs away and waits for me to claim my food, then returns to fixing their plate once I'm finished.

Odd, but then again, they work here, so I suppose it makes sense to have some sort of priority.

I can't help but think about the days on the street that were food scarce, when we had very little to share among ourselves. I have to hand it to Derrek; there was never a day that we didn't have *something* to eat. But there were plenty of days where it wasn't nearly enough to ease the cramping hunger in my belly. Not to mention the dark days in foster care when we were literally not fed at all.

Now, I sit at a table with enough to feed all the kids in Derrek's crew five times over, and the scents that enticed me just a few minutes ago lose their appeal. I force bites of food into my mouth because I took the plate and I don't want it to go to waste, but I've lost my appetite.

This whole place is so much excess. It just doesn't

make sense. A two-hundred room house for one man? This ridiculous amount of food? The guys told me yesterday the population of Smoky Falls is barely over five thousand people. There's no way a mayor here earns enough to keep up a place like this. He must just be hemorrhaging money to keep the place afloat.

Which leads me to wonder *why* he does it.

I observe him while I eat, reading over a sheaf of paper in a folder, making notes in the margins as he sips coffee.

"Uncle Dom?" I ask in what I hope is an innocent tone.

He starts, then looks up with a smile. "Yes, Layla?"

"This house, you said it belongs to our family, right? It's not like a perk of being mayor?"

"Yes, it's been our family home since 1895, I'm afraid."

"Where's the rest of our family?"

His dark brows furrow. "I'm sorry, I don't follow."

"Well, it's hard to imagine they built this giant house for a family of four. There has to be a reason for so many bedrooms, such a large dining room?"

The housekeepers and kitchen staff glance back and forth at each other but don't utter a word, choosing instead to become extremely interested in their plates.

"Yes, well..." Uncle Dom clears his throat. "You have to remember that back in that era, people with a lot of wealth built excessively large houses for multiple reasons. They liked to invite guests to stay, for example, often for several months at a time. Our ancestors might invite a party of thirty people to spend the summer here. It was a part of the culture. People didn't have any of the electronic entertainment we have now, and travel was expensive. So visiting friends was the best way to enjoy society."

"But how big was our family back then?" I press. "How many people actually lived here when the house was built?"

The butler, whose name I've learned is Mr. Carson, clears his throat. "I believe, Sir," he starts in a low gravelly tone, "That the historical book in the library might answer the young lady's questions on Harridan House." He turns to me with a small smile and twinkly eyes. "The builders kept detailed records, and your great-great-grandfather was somewhat of a historian. He put together a delightful book about their life here at the turn of the twentieth century. I can lay it out for you in the library after breakfast, if you like?"

My heart leaps. "Yes, that would be fantastic. Thank you, Mr. Carson."

He nods astutely, then returns his somber gaze to the plate before him.

"Excellent," my uncle says. "Then that should take care of your questions!"

"For now," I agree lightly, surreptitiously studying the rest of the household staff as I continue eating. Mr. Carson would certainly have known my mother, and perhaps Mrs. Dowling the head housekeeper. The rest of them were too young or hadn't been here long enough. Thanks to our chat over cocoa yesterday, I know Susan has been here a decade, and the head chef only two years.

Mrs. Dowling is an imposing woman whose sharp eyes seem to be glued to her watch. The younger housekeepers jump when she walks into the room and flurry around, trying to work quickly and efficiently. She's so precise about how everything is done, I can't help but assume she's been doing this job for a very long time.

Mr. Carson often sports a dour expression and doesn't speak much. However, the hint of a smile when discussing the history book gives me reason to hope he's not as serious as he seems.

As I finish my plate and push away, I decide to start with him.

I feel guilty walking away and leaving my dishes at the table, but I learned last night that it offends the staff if I try to take them to the kitchen myself. Sure enough, before I'm two steps away, the younger red-headed maid hustles over and picks everything up, bussing it into the kitchen.

I have got to hand it to them, they take great pride in their work.

I wander around the ground floor for a while, poking in the nooks and crannies, becoming even more familiar with the house. One thing that strikes me as odd: there's not a single photograph. Anywhere. The house is like a museum, for all you can tell that someone lives here. Perhaps my uncle has photos in his room, or the office. Maybe it's the sort of place they hold a lot of official functions so they keep the personal effects private?

Of course, there are tons of fancy oil paintings all over the building, in every space. But I have yet to see a regular photo. This thought gets my mind churning, and I decide to go on a hunt through the public areas to see if I can find any paintings that might be my mom. Perhaps I've seen some and assumed they were old, but it makes sense that an old money family like this one would have oil portraits done, even in the twentieth century.

I comb through the first floor carefully, but there aren't that many common spaces with portraits. On the second floor I work through all the rooms Uncle Dom showed me, and I see a few of young women with striking dark hair and green eyes, but none that look remotely modern. Would they paint newer portraits with old-fashioned dresses, or were these just old portraits?

Travelling down the long hallway, I notice an odd pattern: There's always a portrait of a young lady, followed by three different men, before another woman. The ladies look similar, all pale-skinned with coifs of dark hair and bright green eyes, the knowing smile on their lips eerily similar to the one I see in the mirror.

The men are incredibly diverse, ranging dramatically in hair colors and skin tones. Always three, following a woman who is clearly my ancestor. I count five sets in all as I traverse the hallways. The clothing styles of the women seem to evolve from corsets and bustles to looser garments, with one featuring a woman with short-cropped hair and the distinctive drop-waisted style of the nineteen twenties. The men wear dapper suits with wide lapels, and the next woman's portrait appears to be set in the fifties. She sits in a stiff-shouldered dress, a belt cinched at her tiny waist with a voluminous skirt that pours over her lap. She styled her dark curls in an elegant bob, and the three men that follow her all wear fashions from the same era.

But after that, the wall stretches down the hall and is completely blank. *What does it mean?*

"Miss?" Mr. Carson's voice startles me.

"Yes?" I jump before turning to face him, heart racing. I can't help the bubbles of guilt that churn in my stomach, despite knowing I am doing nothing wrong.

"I laid out the book I mentioned at breakfast. It's in the library."

"Thank you, Mr. Carson."

He turns to leave, and I have a sudden insight that this could be the time to ask.

"Wait! Mr. Carson, what can you tell me about these portraits?"

He turns slowly on his heel and joins me in front of the last woman. "This is your grandmother, Lorraine Harridan." His eyes are glued to her face, and intuition strikes me.

"She's very elegant," I offer, trying to coax a response.

"She was a very fine woman," he agrees in his grav-elly voice.

"Was? I assume she's passed away?"

"Yes, miss. She's been gone for some time."

"And who are all these men? Are they other family members?"

He hesitates, and when he speaks, the answer comes out awkwardly. "Yes, they were all members of your family, but they're all gone now."

"Aside from my uncle, do I have any other family left? Anywhere in the world?"

"To my knowledge, miss, you and your uncle are all that remain of the Harridan line."

"Thank you, Mr. Carson. I'm curious: since you knew my grandmother, did you know my mother?"

His gaze finally leaves the portrait, and he turns to me with sadness in his watery blue eyes. "I did, miss. I watched her grow up."

"Is any of her stuff still around here, or maybe I could see her room? I feel like I know so little about her."

Once again, he hesitates. "We cleaned her suite of rooms out to redecorate for you, miss. But I believe they moved all of her things to the attic for storage."

My excitement drops, but then rises again at the second half of his statement. "Would it be possible for me to see those things?"

"I'm not sure it would be proper for you to go to the attic..." he looks distinctly uncomfortable, and I certainly don't want him to rat me out just yet.

I rush to ease his distress and throw him off the scent. "Okay, that's fine, thank you very much, Mr.

Carson. I appreciate the information. I'll go check out that book now."

With a relieved sigh, he nods. "Very well, miss, right this way," and gestures down the hallway toward the library.

True to his word, there's a heavy-bound book sitting on the table, conveniently placed before the cushy sofa. As if expecting my needs, Mr. Carson lit a fire in the fireplace, and its warmth has already chased away the chill from the drafty two-story windows.

I settle in and begin flipping through. It's a slick book with glossy pages, clearly made by a publisher. It reads like a coffee-table book with interesting factoids, and plenty of Victorian-style photos of my ancestors.

I study a few portraits of more women who look like me in high-collared dresses with frilly details, examining their stern faces. There are photos of families with dolled-up children and grainy pictures of large parties standing on the lawn in front of the house.

I read the book cover-to-cover, only stopping when Mr. Carson interrupts me with a tray of lunch. I've been so deep in my study of the book that hours have flown by without me even realizing it.

But even before I finish, I know without a doubt that this book is more propaganda than actual history.

For one, it never explains the origin of the family and where they accumulated such wealth. Or why they chose this spot to live and build their mansion.

It also gives no lineage. Sure, they mention a few

names here and there, but mostly, it reads like a fluff piece in a local newspaper. I got more information from Landon and Milo yesterday than I did from this massive 'historical book.'

Frustrated, I slam the cover closed and stare out the window, surprised to realize it's almost nightfall. The rumble in my belly hints, but I check my phone to confirm it's nearly dinner time. Roxanne assured me jeans and a sweater were perfectly fine attire for most nights, so I head downstairs to the breakfast room.

It's empty, so I sit and wait for everyone to arrive.

I'm still sitting at the table alone when the staff brings in dinner.

"Shouldn't I wait for Uncle Dom, or Roxanne?" I ask, confused.

The red-headed maid, Mary, shakes her head. "Oh no, miss, it's just you tonight. The others are in town for a meeting." Seeming to take pity on me, she adds, "We normally have family dinner on Sunday, but I think the... I think Mister Dominic considered the party last night to take its place." She dips her head and scurries back to the kitchen.

My heart drops. No one, not even Roxanne, texted me all day, or even said boo to me since breakfast. Now I'm in this massive and ornate room, with a feast set before me on a table that seats eight, and I'm alone.

My eyes prickle, and the empty room feels cavernous as I shrink into myself. I didn't realize until now how much I've gotten used to Roxanne's constant company in the last year. I thought I was chafing at the bit for freedom, when in fact I was just getting used to being looked after. And clearly the staff here are doing a fine job of looking after me.

But it isn't the same; I'm still lonely.

Deciding, I stand and march into the kitchen. There's a riotous noise as soon as I pass through the door, and my spirits instantly lift. The staff eat their dinner, teasing each other and perched on barstools along the countertop. Mr. Carson and Mrs. Dowling sit at a small breakfast nook in the corner, observing the others like amused parents with bickering children. A smile spreads across my lips; this feels better, more homey. I slip out before they notice me and retrieve my plate, then walk back into the kitchen and step up to an empty seat at the counter.

A stunned silence falls over the group, several of their faces reddening at my presence.

"Miss Layla, is there something wrong with your food?" William, the head chef, looks concerned. He's a bear of a man with a bright ginger beard and the entire chef's outfit, complete with the puffy muffin-looking hat.

"No, not at all! I just… don't want to eat in there by myself. Do you guys mind if I eat in here with you? It's a lot more cozy."

They all look incredibly uncomfortable, like they don't know what to say, and my heart sinks again. *Stupid, Layla.*

"I'm sorry. I don't want to make you uncomfortable. This is your space, I see that now. I won't force myself on you. But if any of you would like, you're welcome to join me in the dining room. It would be my pleasure." I bite my tongue to hold in the tears and collect my plate quietly, retreating to the dining room alone.

Hushed whispers follow me, but I don't understand what they say. I settle back in my seat and prepare for a lonely dinner, letting the tears trickle down my cheeks. Why not? There's no one to witness them, anyway. I'm tempted to text Milo or Landon, but I don't know what to say to them other than whining that I'm lonely and that's definitely not a good look. Since I barely know those guys, it's probably best if I don't dump my negativity all over them just yet. I'm too upset to say anything pleasant to Roxanne right now, and that basically rounds out my contact list.

I'm just picking at my green beans when the kitchen door swings open, and Mr. Carson walks through carrying a plate and a water glass.

"Do you mind if I join you, Miss Layla?" He stands stiff as a board and addresses me formally in his gravelly tone.

My lips curl into a smile, and I swipe a sleeve over my face to dry my cheeks. "Please, have a seat, Mr. Carson."

He sits and begins eating without saying a word. Following his lead, I dig into my dinner with renewed appetite.

We don't exchange words, just eat in silence together. I don't know if he drew the short straw or volunteered to join me.

But either way, I'm extremely grateful for his presence.

Chapter Seven

LAYLA

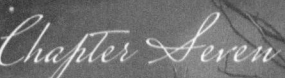

I wake, gasping, and sit up in bed. Once again, I had a wolf dream. But unlike the previous two, this one was terrifying. My heart pounds so hard it feels like it might break through the cage of my chest. Instead of running through the forest with friends, I was fending off attacks from much larger wolves with sharp teeth and vicious claws. I knew they wanted to kill me, and I fought with all my strength.

But I was losing.

I soaked my tank top and shorts in sweat, and the middle of the giant bed where I lay.

Yuck.

I throw back the covers and stumble toward my

closet, grateful for the chill in the air to chase the heat from my skin. My heart slows, and I change into clean pajamas before swiping a bottle of water from my new fridge and returning to bed.

After rearranging the pillows so I have a dry corner to sleep on, I settle back and try to conjure up more details.

There was a clearing in the woods, and wolves of all shapes and sizes surrounded me. I was a wolf, albeit a small one compared to the others. But we were playing like dogs do, frolicking around in the moonlight.

Then three hulking beasts attacked me at once, and none of the other wolves came to help me. They backed away, whimpering, and watched.

I search for anything else, but there's nothing more to recall.

My eyes grow heavy, and I settle back in the soft pillows, reminding myself I have to go to school tomorrow for the first time in four years, and staying up analyzing random dreams is probably not the best way to prepare.

Just as I'm nodding off, I swear I hear the howling of a wolf.

But it's probably just a memory of my dream.

Milo

"Where is she? You're sure she's coming to this class first, right? She should be here by now." Landon is on his tiptoes trying to spot Lex, even though he can see over about 90% of the student population flat-footed.

"Yes, this is her first class," I remind him, tamping down the sarcasm in my tone. I'm as anxious as he is, but I just do better controlling it. "Roxanne sent me her schedule to make sure it matches up with ours. Dom doesn't want anyone messing with her on the first day. The alpha order will stop them from saying anything about our wolves, but he can't actually order people to be nice to her. And you know how it's probably going to go."

Landon's worried expression hardens. "Yeah, I know. I just... should we have met her at the door? How is she getting to school, anyway? Are we sure she can find her way here?"

"Maxwell is driving her and it's a straight shot from the front door, man. She isn't a moron, she can figure it out." Despite my reassurances to Landon, I can feel the tension running through my body. I consciously relax my fists and draw in a deep breath. "We're supposed to help her find her way around and make her comfortable, Landon. Not stress her the fuck out. So chill, alright?"

He swipes a hand through his hair, blind to the appraising glances of passing girls. "Alright, alright. I hear you. I just can't help it. We've waited so long, and then being around her Saturday-"

"I know, man, but you've gotta be chill or she's not going to *want* to be around us. We don't want to creep her out. We may know she's our fated, but *she* doesn't know that yet."

He pulls in a deep breath and breathes it out slowly. "You're right. Okay. When does she meet Jared?"

"He doesn't have morning classes on Monday, lucky asshole. So he's going to meet us for lunch. He's in her English Lit class this afternoon."

"I can't wait to see his face when he—oh, there she is, I see her!" He practically shouts and several people walking past stare at us.

"Dude, chill. Be cool or I swear to god I'm going to kick your ass so hard it'll take you a week to recover."

"I'm cool, alright?" Landon sighs, shoving his hands in his pockets and leans against the wall. He may have height on me, but he knows I'm a better fighter and I don't threaten violence lightly. Lex is our fated, we can't screw it up.

Finally, I can see her now. She's tiny, but her wild dark hair gives her several inches of height and I could pick her out of a crowd easily. The sensation of electricity zipping across my skin grows stronger, alerting me to her presence. As if I didn't already know.

Her gaze is down, focused on her phone screen as she pinches her fingers and widens them, clearly trying to zoom in on something. Likely a map of the school.

"Layla!" Landon shouts, waving his long-ass arms in the air and grinning like an idiot. "Layla, over here!"

I punch him in the ribs and he drops his arms, huffing out an "ow!"

But his stunt works. It gets her attention, and she's heading our way with a tentative smile.

She's obviously put a little effort into her appearance today. Even though her hair is still wild, she's got some purple shadow on her lids and her pale complexion is even more dewy than Saturday. She also has a berry-colored lip gloss on that makes her mouth deliciously tempting. I try not to stare directly at it when I speak.

"Hey Lex," I give her my best 'charming devil' smile and make direct eye contact. "Nice to see you again."

"Yeah, you guys too. Did you have a good weekend?" Her eyes dart to Landon, who's grinning at her like a jackass.

I give him an elbow to the ribs so he knocks it off. "Yeah, it was okay. You?"

"Okay. I just hung out at the castle with the serving dishes," she snorts sarcastically. "Read a book. Nothing too exciting."

"What book? Anything interesting?"

"A History of Harridan House." She rolls her eyes. "It was gripping."

A chuckle passes my lips. "Yes, sounds engrossing."

A few seconds too late, Landon barks an exaggeratedly loud laugh.

I gesture for Lex to head into the classroom. "Ladies first."

She smiles again and turns toward the door, and I punch Landon even harder in the ribs. "Dude, what the fuck?" I hiss under my breath. "You're acting completely insane!"

Landon winces from the punch and drags his hands over his face. "I knooooooow! But it's like I can't help myself. My heart is beating a mile a minute and I just feel giddy around her. I'm like a kid at freaking Disney World. I don't know what to do with myself."

We walk into the classroom slowly and follow Lex up to an empty row of seats in the lecture hall.

"Well, you'd better figure it out quick. Got it?"

He nods and takes the seat to Lex's left while I claim the one to the right.

She busies herself with getting a notebook and pen out of her small backpack, and Landon and I quickly do the same, although I don't expect to be taking many notes. More students filter in, and I catch many pairs of eyes landing on Lex with curiosity. Fortunately, no one we're worried about is in this class, so we won't have to fend off any attacks for this hour.

The next class, however…

I'm just leaning over to ask Lex about LA when the professor walks in, throws his briefcase on the front table with a bang, and shouts, "Welcome to Intro to American History. I'm sure you all *love* the early Monday class as much as I do, so as long as we respect each other's time and caffeine addictions, I think we'll get along just fine. Agreed?"

A tittering laugh runs through the room and the professor raises his travel mug in salute.

I settle back in my seat and prepare for a history lecture from a prof who obviously thinks he's a 'cool teacher.'

This is going to be a long hour.

Chapter Eight

LAYLA

❧

I admit, it's nice walking into the building and being greeted as if I have actual friends on the first day of class. I was so nervous that it would be a repeat of the nightmare of starting high school. I almost bailed completely, then settled for spending an hour selecting my outfit.

Starting freshman year as a foster kid when my parents had just died was about as close to hell as it gets. We never had a lot of money growing up, but I at least got new school clothes when my parents were alive. Not only did that not happen, but I went through a growth spurt that summer and most of my clothes were embarrassingly short or tight. My curves came in from nowhere and suddenly nerdy, nose-in-a-book Layla became labeled a slut day one.

Now I have more clothes than I could have fathomed a year ago. After the excruciating selection process, I'm relieved to walk into the school and see most of the girls are dressed somewhat similar to me in distressed, straight-legged jeans and cropped sweaters. People glance at me curiously, but no one is openly hostile, which definitely helps my confidence.

Then I hear Landon's voice and see him waving both arms at me, smiling brightly. My heart skips a beat —even in a basic sweater and jeans combo, he's distractingly hot with those piercing eyes and full lips. Something about his height makes me want to run and jump into his arms just to see if he'd catch me. The electric chills of attraction resurface the closer I get to them, and I drag my lip between my teeth to distract myself.

Of course, Milo is beside Landon, his wardrobe even sharper. I'm starting to think Milo has a bit of a hipster style, and although it's never been my thing I'm kind of digging it. He's wearing khakis, but they're slim fit and cuffed casually at the ankle, displaying black shoes that match his black v-neck t-shirt. Several necklaces dangle on his chest at varying lengths; interesting, industrial-looking metal pieces strung on strips of dark brown leather. I wonder if they have any meaning or he just thinks they look cool.

They greet me and we exchange a few words, although I barely pay attention. I'm too nervous, there's so many firsts to keep track of today and I don't want to screw up. First day at a new school, first day of college, first class, *first class with incredibly hot friends that make my skin tingle…*

Eventually we go inside and claim seats, and I do my best to copy down notes even though I'm hopelessly distracted by the two of them. A cloud of their combined fragrance envelopes me; Milo has a woodsy cedar scent, and Landon's is lighter, more citrusy. The two scents don't clash, and in fact smell quite pleasant together. I sit ramrod straight, consciously avoiding leaning either way to get a better whiff.

Besides their scent, I feel their eyes on me constantly. I never catch them looking, but energy ripples across my skin, the hairs on my neck rising repeatedly. At one point, I swear Landon leans over and just takes a long breath, as if he's *smelling me.*

Glad to see I'm not the only one with that desire.

By the end of class, I still haven't decided if I'm flattered or disturbed by the attention.

Either way, I'm grateful that I'm not alone.

"Well, I dunno about you guys, but that's definitely going to be something I'm looking forward to, first thing in the morning, three days a week," Milo mutters as we file out of class.

"You don't like history?" I glance up at him curiously.

"It's not that. I'm just annoyed by Professor Barker. His whole, 'I'm not a regular teacher, I'm a *cool* teacher,' thing is going to get old, fast."

I snort a laugh. "You may have a point. But what if that's just his personality? Maybe he's just a realist?"

Milo's lips curl into a sardonic grin. "We'll see."

"So, Layla, what's your next class?" Landon pipes up from my other side.

"Erm," I check the schedule on my phone. "I have Bio 103 with Calhoun."

"Cool, me too! I'll show you the way. We all had freshman orientation last week, so I know the campus pretty well. See you at lunch, Milo."

"Yeah, I'll meet you guys in front of the cafeteria. Jared is supposed to find me after my class."

"Who's Jared?" I glance between their faces. This is the first time they've mentioned him.

"He's our other… friend. We're kind of like the three musketeers," Landon jokes, but I don't miss how he tripped over the word 'friend.'

Huh. *Were they not actually friends?* "I see. Okay, we'll see you at lunch, Milo."

He hits me with that sexy half-grin again. "See ya Lex."

Landon leads, and I follow him from the main building across the courtyard to the Donnager building, where the science and math classes are held. Science has never been my strong suit—I've always preferred litera-ture—but it's a requirement, so I have to get it done at some point, might as well be now.

We pick a black-topped table near the back, and I set out my notebook and pens. We're not chatting, but it's a companionable silence. I'm getting the impression that

Landon is a little more introverted than Milo, and I kind of like it. Milo has his whole cool confidence going on, but I'm definitely an introvert, so I'm far more likely to be awkward than cool. It's nice that Landon is the same.

I'm minding my business, writing the name of the class and the date on the first page of my notebook, when a nasal voice sneers, "So it's true, Smoky Falls has a brand new princess."

That fucking nickname again.

I try not to overreact and glance up casually. A pretty blonde girl, wearing a nearly identical outfit to mine, stands in front of our table. She's flanked by two large guys, twins from the looks of it, with reddish-brown hair. They're all glaring at me with marked dislike, perhaps even hate, clear on their faces. Why, I have no earthly idea, but people rarely make sense to me.

There's a low rumbling sound to my right, and I realize Landon is actually growling—*growling!*—deep in his chest. *What in the...*

Thankfully, I know how to deal with bitchy girls. A few years on the streets gave me a pretty thick skin, and there's nothing a rich teenage girl likes better than picking on a poor girl. I guess, technically I am a rich girl now, judging by my uncle's mansion and all the new possessions I can claim as my own. However, that doesn't stop my hackles from rising to the challenge.

Deciding to play it cool, I flip my hair and glance at them with casual disinterest. "Oh, don't worry about me, blondie, I'm not after your title."

An immediate rumble circulates the room as my classmates react. I didn't realize until now that they are all watching this little showdown.

"You say that, and yet you're here all the same," she sniffs. "You should never have come here, Harridan."

Wait, how does this bitch know who I am? And what the hell is her problem?

"Okay, stalker. I don't know what business it is of yours what I do, but I'm just here for an education like everyone else. So why don't you flounce back to your seat with your bulldogs and mind your business?"

"Yeah, no one believes that. But we'll deal with you soon enough."

Landon slams his hands down on the table, arms trembling and face red with restrained rage. The sudden motion and loud noise make me jump, along with half the class. "That's *enough*, Amber. Take your lackeys and get out of my face before we have a *problem*."

He seems to have a secondary implication besides the obvious, but I have no idea what it could be. However, his intervention works, and Amber sniffs once more before turning on her heel and marching away, followed by her bodyguards.

"I'm sorry about that," Landon leans in to whisper, his warm breath tickling my ear. "I should have stopped her earlier."

I turn to him with a smile. "It's alright, I'm used to dealing with assholes. I'm just surprised it took this long to meet one," I joke. "Not sure what I did to piss her off, though. You think it's because she doesn't like to be twinsies?" Amber's cardigan is nearly the same as mine, in a baby pink color instead of lavender.

Landon snorts. "Maybe, maybe not. Either way, I know you can probably handle yourself, but the point is you don't have to. You have Milo and me now, and Jared. If Milo were here, he'd probably have sent her off with her tail between her legs before she got a word out, but," he ducks his head, cheeks reddening, "I'm not as direct as he is."

My heart lurches for him, and I place a hand on his arm. "I disagree. I appreciate that you let me deal with it myself, and then came in when she didn't get the hint. You certainly sent her running fast," I giggle. "Truth time: are your palms killing you? That slap was loud."

He chuckles. "Yeah, to be honest, they do kind of sting. It's okay, it'll go away in a few minutes."

"I thought you were going to crack the table," I add in a stage-whisper. "Remind me not to get on your bad side."

Instantly, Landon's gaze becomes hooded and intense. My heart rate rises in response to some physiological cue I can't see, the electricity crackling between us again.

"You could never get on my bad side, Layla."

A loud bang makes us jump apart, and I glance forward to see the professor has closed the door. What is it with the teachers and their dramatic entrances here?

"Welcome to Bio 103, class. I'm Professor Calhoun. I hope you like the person you're sitting next to. They will be your best friend for this semester in both Monday lecture and lab Thursday afternoons."

Landon turns to me with a giant, cheery grin, eyes sparkling, and my heart melts a little.

If he's going to keep looking at me like that, I may not hate Bio after all.

Chapter Nine

LAYLA

~

Even though the professor's lecture is absolute gibberish to me, it seems I'm fortunate in my choice of lab partner because Landon has no problem explaining the lesson to me, this time in words I understand.

The odd incident with the girl Landon called Amber and her twin bodyguards has completely slipped my mind by the time class is over, but I'm reminded of it when she turns around to glare hatefully at me before exiting the class.

"Seriously?" I mutter, shoving things into my backpack.

"What?" Landon looks up, confused.

"Nothing. I just caught that girl glaring at me again.

You don't have any idea why she hates me so much, do you?"

"Erm, I'm not exactly an expert on girl stuff," he coughs awkwardly. "I dunno about you, but I'm starving. Milo and Jared should be waiting for us, lets go get some lunch."

The feeling that he's not telling me something is hard to ignore, but I don't know how to press him. It's entirely possible he just doesn't like to speak ill of anyone. I don't know him well enough to understand all of his moods quite yet.

We walk across campus, with Landon pointing out various buildings he recognizes from the tour I was too late to receive. I sort of listen to him and sort of watch the other students we pass.

About half pay no attention to me at all.

Most that pay attention give me an appraising look, or seem genuinely excited to see me, a complete stranger, which is definitely odd.

But even more odd are the few decidedly unfriendly looks. Given that it's the first day of class, I'd assumed a solid quarter of the students would start out new and anonymous, just like me, while upper classmen might know each other and already have friends. Perhaps some kids from the local town might attend together and carry over any friendships or prejudices from high school.

But what on earth could that possibly have to do with me?

My skin crawls with the knowledge that there's

more here than meets the eye. I wish I had more concrete proof than a creepy feeling, but that feeling has served me plenty well on the streets, and I've always trusted it. Even in the foster home, it warned me when there was danger coming my way.

In fact, I first noticed it not long after my parents died. It was as if an instinct for self preservation sprung into life, with an internal voice warning me of danger and deceit.

Right now Landon still pings as familiar and safe, but I know he's not telling me something. So I follow him to the cafeteria, but keep my eyes open for trouble.

As promised, Milo is waiting outside the glass doors with another guy. This one falls between Landon and Milo in height, but is far more muscular. A white t-shirt sets his gleaming dark skin off. It strains at his wide shoulders and matches the brilliant smile that breaks across his face when he spots us.

"Layla, this is Jared," Landon begins as we approach. "Jared, this is-"

"Layla," my name rolls off his tongue with a distinct Tennessee accent I'm beginning to recognize. He grasps my hand and shakes it gently. "It's a pleasure to meet you, gorgeous."

"Nice to meet you," I reply, flushing with pleasure at the compliment and feeling the now-familiar sizzle of electricity across my skin at the contact. Jared's eyes are so dark I can barely distinguish the iris from his pupils, but they gaze upon me with warmth, and an intensity that brings more heat to my cheeks.

"Are you hungry? We've got an hour before English 101." He gestures to the cafeteria door that Milo is holding open.

"How did you know I have English 101 next?" I raise my eyebrows in surprise.

"Busted!" Landon laughs and Milo shakes his head.

Jared looks at his feet guiltily. "Roxanne, Dom's... assistant, is my auntie. She told us your schedule so you wouldn't be alone on your first day."

"Oh, I see." My warm fuzzy feelings at their flattering attention dissipate immediately. So they were just instructed to keep me company? Annoyance floods my system to replace the disappointment. "Well, in that case, thanks, but no thanks. I'm not a charity case. I don't need a hired escort." I stomp through the doors and leave them scrambling in my wake.

I swipe my student ID card and gain access to the overwhelming food options before the three of them catch up to me.

"Layla, look-" Landon joins me in the salad line.

"No thanks, Landon. It's hard enough to be the new kid without the added embarrassment of having someone *assigned* to keep me company. I'd rather be on my own."

"No, really, it's not-"

"Just leave me alone," I swipe a packaged salad and march off, finding a slice of pepperoni pizza and a drink before I claim a seat at an empty table.

My stomach is roiling with humiliation. Of course, it wasn't so simple as a trio of hot guys just wanted to be my friends… *or more,* the helpful little voice in my head whispers in disappointment. Leave it to Roxanne to force them to escort me around. I pick morosely at my salad with my head down, and mentally draft a dozen angry text messages to her about the indignity.

Of course, that isn't the end. I hear all three of them slide into seats around me, and a heavy sigh escapes my lips.

"Guys, I'll tell Roxanne we're all besties, okay? Whatever she promised you, you'll get it. I just don't want or need your pity. I'll be fine."

"Well, maybe if you'd let us get a word in edge-wise before dismissing us again, you might find out that's not the case," Milo says from my right with a wry smile.

"Go on." My brows lower and I glare at him, daring him to change my mind.

"What Jared *meant* to say is that we *asked* Roxanne for your schedule after we ran into you on Saturday. We didn't want to sound like stalkers, which is why Jared left that bit out. But I promise, no one forced us to hang out with you. We want to be here, if that's okay with you."

I hold his gaze for a long moment, but his eyes betray nothing besides sincerity and I have to conclude it isn't a lie.

"Fine," I sniff, straightening, and picking up my slice. "But don't try to pull one over on me, ever. I can tell when people are lying."

The three guys exchange a long look, then drop their focus to their food without a word. Before I question it, a girl with long, wavy brown hair slides into the empty seat beside me.

"Hi! You're new, right? I'm Savannah. Welcome to Smoky Falls!" Her eyes are startlingly blue and energy pours off her in waves, charging the atmosphere like an oncoming storm.

I swallow my food. "Hi, Savannah, I'm Layla." For some reason, I've fallen out of the habit of using my street name when I meet new people, and sort of regret telling Milo to call me Lex. I wonder if I could get him to change it? It doesn't seem to fit into my new environment.

"Layla Harridan, right?" Savannah's wide grin is infectious, and I can't help returning it.

"Yeah, that's right. How did you know?"

"Oh," she laughs lightly, "Small town. Word gets around. But it's so nice to meet you!"

"Thanks, you too. You're the first girl I've met outside of Harridan House. Well, aside from Amber," I spit her name with distaste. "But you're definitely more friendly than she was."

Savannah's cheerful grin falls slightly. "Oh… well, don't worry about her. She's not very nice in general. Some people think the world owes them something, and they hand their grudges down to their kids. It has nothing to do with you."

"What grudge does Amber's family have against me?"

"Nothing serious, I'm sure," Milo interrupts smoothly with a pointed look at Savannah. "It's pretty well known that her family has always been jealous of the Harridan's wealth. Why, I have no idea, they have plenty of money. But some people always want more."

"Okay," I eye him suspiciously. I like Milo, but he's very careful with his choice of words, almost as if he knows to avoid telling me a lie.

Which, to be fair, I did just warn him against. But most people don't take that warning seriously.

Milo, apparently, does.

In another flurry of activity, more people join our table and introduce themselves to me excitedly. I'm swiftly overwhelmed with names in the face of my sudden popularity, and the day continues in the same vein. A small amount of unfriendly glances are sent my way, interspersed with waves of happy individuals who can't wait to make my acquaintance. They all seem to know me, or at least know of me, and I can only conclude that some kind of word went around that the mayor's niece arrived in Smoky Falls.

After his initial apparent screw up, Jared seems extra careful to avoid putting his foot in his mouth again and barely says two words to me during English. Maxwell is picking me up promptly after class, and Jared escorts me to the front. I want to make him comfortable but I don't know what to say to the guy, I hardly know him. My phone has been buzzing throughout class, but I have a feeling I know who it is and I'm not in the mood. I thank Jared for walking with me, and utter a low goodbye before I slide into the back of the dark-tinted car.

"Did you have a good day, Miss Layla?" Maxwell asks in a neutral voice as we drive away.

"I suppose so." I really don't know how to answer him, but it seems reasonably accurate.

Apparently that's the extent of his interest, because he doesn't follow up with any more questions and I volunteer nothing on the long, winding drive to Harridan House.

Chapter Ten

LAYLA

~

"We're doing *what* tonight?" my gaze flicks back and forth between Landon and Milo, sure I didn't hear them right.

After a long week of learning my way around campus, always escorted by one of the three guys and often accompanied by more of our lunchtime crowd, I'm kind of peopled-out. I'm actually looking forward to a quiet night in my castle like a proper princess, curled up in front of a roaring fire with a good book. Even though the weather has been temperate in Smoky Falls, Harridan House is a good drive up the mountain from town, and the temperature here always seems a good twenty degrees cooler. The leaves have barely begun to change and I'm already having fantasies about frolicking in the snow with furry woodland creatures,

So far today I've been schlubbing around the cool house in sweats. In Smoky Falls, my wardrobe leans decidedly on the 'late summer' side of my closet, although I haven't been able to bring myself to bare my arms around my new friends. Even though I don't mind the silvery scars, I know people will have tons of questions, and I just don't want something else that sets me apart from my peers. Having to explain how my teen years were spent living on the streets, let alone the subsequent attack that left me sliced to ribbons, is not high on my list of 'want to share'.

However, the guys turned up at my doorstep, Mr. Carson let them in, and they are now excitedly trying to drag me from the house in my sweatpants.

"It's the first football game of the year! The Smoky Falls Wolves are hosting the Southtown Bears."

"So?"

"So, we have to go support Jared. He's in the starting lineup." Landon looks at me as if I'm crazy.

Okay, so I get that I'm supposed to be into supporting the school at sporting events because that is some kind of college experience. I've just never grown up in an environment that encouraged it, so organized sports are not something I've ever cared about.

"Is that a big deal?"

Landon gapes at me, but Milo smacks him in the arm and his jaw snaps shut.

"For a freshman to be on the starting lineup is a big deal," Milo explains with a smile. "And it would be a big deal to Jared if you came to support him."

"I dunno. I don't think he really cares much about what I think."

"Of course he cares! What makes you think he doesn't?"

"He barely talks to me." I shrug. "I text with you guys every day, but aside from when he sent me his number, I haven't gotten another message from him."

Milo and Landon exchange glances. "He's... well, I wouldn't say he's shy," Landon explains. "But trust me, he likes you. He just needs time to get to know you, is all. I think you kind of intimidate him."

"Well, I'm not sure I'm particularly interested in chasing down some guy who's not all that interested in getting to know *me*," I sniff, but my feelings are slightly mollified at the idea that I intimidate him. Jared, the ripped, super popular football player that's on the starting lineup, finds *me* intimidating?

"I promise you that's not the case." Milo's eyes bore into mine, radiating sincerity. "He's just sensitive, and the truth is... he feels bad that he made you think Roxanne ordered us to hang out with you."

"But we cleared all of that up?"

Landon snorts. "Yeah, well, Jared isn't the type to get over that stuff easily. Once you get to know him, it's impossible to shut him up, I swear. But it will mean a lot to him for you to come to the game. And we'll have a good time, I promise. There's junk food and the band plays and... well, you know."

A worm of discomfort wriggles in my stomach. I don't correct him, but I don't *really* know. I've seen high school football games portrayed on tv. Surely some small community college game would be similar?

"Alright, fine, I'll go. Let me get changed."

"Here," Landon holds out a plastic bag and I open it, confused. It has a football jersey inside.

I glance up at him with one raised brow. "And?"

"That's Jared's jersey."

"Won't he need it?"

"It's his *away* jersey. The team has two different sets. It's a thing that they can allow someone to wear their other jersey during the game. Jared asked us to bring it to you, if you want to wear it."

Warmth spreads through my chest. This seems like a boyfriend-girlfriend sort of thing, and I find it amusing that both Landon and Milo are helping. Is he really *that* interested?

I've been trying to sort out what these guys are after all week and I find the entire thing a bit confusing. They're all nice, and sweet, and flirtatious in their own ways. Are they interested in me, or just being friendly?

Regardless, the gesture with the jersey shows Jared cares more about me than he lets on, despite how little he's spoken since we met.

"Okay," I shrug, my emotions in turmoil despite my outwardly placid appearance. "I don't have any school-branded gear anyway, and if I'm going to cheer, I suppose I ought to represent."

Landon beams at me and Milo's customary half-smile returns.

"I'll be right back. You two stay here." I leave them to argue over Netflix and retreat to my bedroom, slipping into the closet to change. After some thought, I pull on jeans and a super-thin, long-sleeved white cotton shirt, then hang the enormous white and blue jersey over the top. I'm absolutely drowning in it, but if this is the 'thing' everyone does, I can't imagine it would fit another girl better. After a quick stop in the bathroom to run a brush through my hair and swipe on some mascara, I present myself to the waiting boys.

"Am I doing this right?" I lift my arms to showcase the oversized jersey, which hangs pretty close to my knees.

Landon snorts a laugh, and Milo stands from the couch to approach me.

"Here, let me try something." He pulls the two edges of the shirt together and knots them at my waist.

My heart beats faster at his proximity, watching his deft fingers tug at my clothing.

"Now you can tuck the back up into your waistband and just let it blouse in the back. At least, that's how the girls were wearing them last fall. But we can always adjust if we see a better option," he adds with a wink.

I do as instructed, and model the new styling for his critical gaze.

"Yep, much better," Milo nods. "What do you think, Landon?"

The other boy grins, his gaze lingering on my lower half for just a beat longer than necessary. "Definitely better. You ready to go?"

"Yeah, let me just grab a... purse or something." I dart back into my closet and dig out a small crossbody bag that's little more than a phone holder with an attached wallet and skinny strap. I transfer my stuff into the purse, and once my phone is situated, I'm ready to go.

"Hey, how much cash do you guys think I'll need? Like, to get in and buy food and stuff?" I ask as I walk back into my suite.

The guys turn to me with horrified expressions. "You don't need any. We've got it covered."

Heat rises to my cheeks. "Oh, it's okay. Roxanne gave me some money and told me I get a weekly allowance for these types of things. Well, 'entertainment' is what she said, but I'm assuming that's the category this falls under."

In fact, I'm kind of proud to have money that I didn't steal, despite feeling slightly weird at the concept of 'allowance'. Just being handed money for existing, to use on whatever I want, is still a bizarre concept for me. Roxanne already told me not to use it on clothes or anything for school. She'd buy me whatever I want or need. This is just... 'fun' money. Another strange concept I'm trying to adapt to.

"Your money's no good tonight." Milo crosses his

arms over his chest with conviction. "We invited you, so we're treating. End of story."

"So if I ask you guys to do something, then I pay?" I'm still struggling with these societal norms. On the street, if someone gives you something, they expect something in return. I don't trust it.

"Sure." Landon winks and wraps an arm around my shoulders. He's wearing a blue and white 'Smoky Falls Wolves' t-shirt with jeans, and we match pretty well.

But when my gaze travels back to Milo, I realize he's not exactly rocking the school colors. Milo is wearing a black v-neck shirt and dark wash jeans, cuffed, with loafers.

I tip my head at him curiously. "Don't you need to change? You don't look very 'school spirit' like the rest of us."

Milo barks a laugh. "No, Lex, I'm not really the school spirit type. I go to support Jared, but I don't do the matchy-matchy outfit. No one doubts which team I'm representing."

Before I can ask another question, Landon steers me toward the door with a gentle push. "Come on, I want to get good seats, and I'm hungry."

"Coffee first," Milo adds. "You know I don't drink that swill at the game." We head toward the elevator at the end of the hall.

"Fine, we'll get coffee first, but that means we're grabbing food in town, too. My backpack is in my car. We can smuggle in Badger's instead of the shitty hotdogs at the concession stand."

"Badgers?" I cannot suppress the look of disgust on my face at the idea of eating a badger. What would that even taste like? Are they actually good to eat?

Landon and Milo exchange a glance and burst into laughter that echoes through the empty hallway. Something tells me I assumed wrong.

"Badger's Burgers," Milo explains. "It's our favorite spot to get a quick meal. I forget you haven't seen much of the town. Maybe after the game, or tomorrow, we can give you a proper tour. The best coffee shop is the Painted Moose. There are a couple other places, but that one has the best espresso roast. Or drip coffee, if that's your jam."

"Sounds good," I reply, and pull the elevator gate shut before mashing the down button. Even though they practically had to drag me out of my sweatpants and couch plans, I'm actually excited about the prospect of going into town for food and a football game.

It's precisely this kind of normalcy that I always longed for. Growing up in LA, much less being a teenage runaway on the streets, makes it easy to believe that these sorts of things only exist in sitcoms.

And yet here I am, living a piece of Americana in jeans and a borrowed football jersey, planning to spend my Saturday afternoon like any other eighteen-year-old girl in college: surrounded by friends and classmates, eating junk food, and cheering for our school team.

When we climb into Landon's white SUV, Milo allows me to take the front seat. The scars on my arms itch to remind me of how I ended up here, and I rub them absentmindedly through my shirt. I think about the change of my fortune that attack wrought, what I went through and how I landed here. Given the choice of staying on the street or what happened to me, I know without any doubt I'd take the pain and physical therapy all over again if it meant I ended up here after all was said and done.

It was absolutely worth it.

Chapter Eleven

LAYLA

~

We visit the Painted Moose first, which is a cute little rustic cabin-themed coffee shop with wildly colored moose outlines hung from the walls. Landon called in our order to Badger's, so our burgers and fries are ready to go when we arrive. Smuggled safely inside Landon's backpack, our meal makes it to the stands where we enjoy the greasy goodness without interruption. We are early and get a magnificent spot, or so Landon assures me.

"You don't want to be too close to the band. It gets really loud. And you don't want to be in the seats closest to the field because people walk past there all the time and interrupt the view, but you don't want to be on the top either, 'cuz then it's hard to see well. Right in the middle is the best spot," he finishes smugly.

Unfortunately, it's also right in the baking afternoon sun. While there was a nice chill in the air in the mountains, here I'm roasting in my dual-layer outfit and full-length jeans.

As if in tune to my feelings—or he can just see the sweat pouring down my face—Landon asks, "Are you too warm, Lex?"

"The sun is pretty hot, and I didn't bring a scrunchie." I lift the heavy weight of my frizzy hair from my back, but there's no breeze to cool off my sweaty neck.

"The game doesn't start for another half hour. Why don't you go take off your long-sleeved shirt? Milo and I will hold your spot. We can get you another drink too, if you're thirsty?"

I cringe internally. Somehow, I knew this was coming. I consider just taking off the jersey, but that isn't a good option—Jared asked me to wear it and there's clearly some significance to it. I chose the thin shirt because it is the lightest long-sleeve I have, but it's also see-through, so I can't wear it on its own unless I feel like displaying my polka-dot bra to the entire crowd. But most importantly, I don't want to take it off and reveal my arms and open myself to the questions.

"It's okay, I'll be fine." I shrug it off like no big deal, but my face is burning and I can just imagine how red it must be.

Milo watches me with a flat expression while I try to be nonchalant.

"What is it?" His voice is demanding, not really a question.

"What is what?" I feign innocence.

"You're not telling me the truth. You're hiding something. What is it?"

I release a half-hearted laugh as if he's crazy, but glancing at Landon, I see his expression is just as serious. No one is sitting close enough to hear yet, and my heart beats wildly when I decide I might as well tell them.

"It's not a big deal, okay? Just... when my uncle found out about me, it was because I'd been attacked. And I have scars on my arms, and I don't want everyone to see them and ask about them."

Milo's dark eyes appear to flash in the bright afternoon light. "Will you show us? Maybe they aren't that bad."

"Oh, they're bad alright," I mutter, but tug the cuff on my sleeve up half way so they can see the silvery lines that run parallel down my arm.

Landon whistles low between his teeth, and he and Milo share a glance. "Do you know what did that?"

I raise an eyebrow. "It wasn't a *what*, it was a *who*. And no, we don't know who it was. The guy who caught him attacking me ran off."

"Is that... all he did? Cut your arms like that?"

Heat pulses in my chest as I pick up on his implication. "He stabbed me in the chest with some kind of metal spike, or so the report says. I've got a nice scar there, too." My voice is defensive but I can't help it. I hunch over my lap, as if preparing to protect myself from an attack.

Milo grasps my arm gently, tugging it from the safe space wrapped around my belly, and turns my wrist left and right to catch bright sunlight on the scars. Finally, he sets it gently back in my lap.

His eyes are intense, but his expression gentle when he uses a finger to tip up my chin. "I'm sorry that happened to you, but I'm not sorry you're here now, with us. You don't have anything to be ashamed of. You clearly survived something terrible, and that just shows how strong you are. No one will say anything."

"Yeah, and if they do, we'll shut them up real quick," Landon adds.

They are definitely responding better than I thought they would, but my heart is still racing. "Are you sure? Honestly the heat's not that bad, and I'm sure it'll cool off-"

"I'm sure, Lex. I just want you to be comfortable, and right now you look anything but."

My eyes dart between the two guys, who wear matching expressions of conviction.

It *would* be amazing to strip off this sweaty shirt and catch the light breeze on my arms...

"Okay," I stand abruptly, trying to look more convinced than I feel. "You're right. I shouldn't be so afraid of showing my skin that I die of heatstroke. Where is the bathroom?"

"I'll take you." Milo stands and gestures down the stairs. "Landon will save our seats, and I'll get us some more drinks while we're down there. Landon, you want anything?"

"Yeah, see if they have that lemonade monster. And you'd better grab a Laffy Taffy for Jared. You know they always sell out."

"Got it," Milo replies. "Come on, Lex, this way."

We navigate out of the bleachers and back through the waves of people heading toward the stands. It's getting crowded, and Milo grabs my hand to keep us together, which spikes my heart rate again as the electricity passes over my skin. Even though I've always leaned more toward the bad boy type with the leather jacket, I find Milo incredibly alluring. His refusal to 'fit in' by wearing a school fan costume gives me that delicious taste of rebellion, even though he's dressed more like a professor than a student.

A young, hot professor, but still—it's not normally my type. There's just something appealing about him. Perhaps it's his cool confidence that I find so attractive. The skin on my palm continues to tingle as we walk, seemingly connected directly to the wild butterflies in my stomach.

Milo leads me straight to the restroom entrance and lets me know he's going to the concession stand while I strip off the sweat-soaked long sleeve and pull the jersey back on. I do a passably good job of retying the front and tucking the back, and emerge feeling about fifty percent cooler.

Only to walk directly into Amber.

She's flanked by a couple of girls I've seen her with before—seriously, does this chick always need two lackeys?—and they all don immediate looks of disgust when they recognize me. Their eyes run over my body as if scrutinizing every inch of me and my outfit, but I have no idea what they could possibly judge since we're all dressed similarly in oversized jerseys and jeans.

"Well, look who it is," Amber sneers. "Already have the jersey on, huh? You move fast."

I glare at her, crossing my arms over my chest, and shrug dismissively. "Jared asked me to wear it, and I saw no reason to say no. But I'm not sure what your problem is since you clearly have your own. Unless you're jealous about this *particular* jersey?"

"Dude, look at her arms!" One lackey squeals, her eyes narrowed hatefully. "Those look like suicide scars —that's a hell of a lot of cuts to *still* fail, Harridan. You must be a special kind of stupid."

Amber's eyes are bright with amusement at the fresh ammunition. "That would explain a lot. Clearly, Jared feels sorry for such a basket case, and Milo and Landon are right there with him. Pity is a powerful motivator."

"Actually," Milo's rich voice rings out from behind them, "she survived an assault by some kind of vicious *beast*, Amber. I'd say Lex here is a lot tougher than you think. Perhaps you'd better run along before she shows you." He slides in beside me and hands me a frosty cup.

"Here you go, babe," he murmurs with a soft press of lips to my temple, sending electric tingles shooting straight to my belly.

"You look hot," he adds, warm breath tickling my temple, before he settles his arm around my hip and turns to Amber with a smirk.

Red creeps up the side of Amber's neck, pooling in her cheeks before her expression changes abruptly from fury to a flirtatious smile. "We should probably go get our seats, girls. See you later, Milo," she adds in a saucy tone.

They step around us and walk away as if we don't exist at all.

"Are you okay?" Milo's low voice is concerned, and his arm raises from my waist to wrap around my shoulders and steer me toward the bleachers.

"Yeah, I'm okay. It figures that bitch would be the first person I run into when I take my shirt off. Seriously, what did I do to her?" I draw a sip of my drink, which is an icy lemonade slushy and ridiculously refreshing.

Milo sighs. "She... kind of has a thing for Jared. For all of us, really. She doesn't like that we're all... hanging out."

My heart sinks. Why is the mean girl drama always about boys?

But his statement sends a wriggle of discomfort through my stomach. Are we *only* hanging out? Is there something more here, or am I just making myself believe it?

I ask carefully, "It's not like I'm dating any of you, so I'm not the reason you're not dating her... right?"

He clears his throat, obviously uncomfortable. "Yeah, she knows that. We just never were interested in her, so I guess the fact that we're hanging out with any girl is bad enough."

Hmm. There's clearly more to this story than he's telling, but it's starting to make more sense why this girl hated me from day one. If she's got a thing for these guys and they're not interested, then I show up and they're always with me. That definitely makes me a target.

By this point, we're climbing back up the bleachers, and the teams are charging out onto the field. I do my best to cheer and support Jared, and more than once I see the player in the jersey with the same number as mine turn and search for us in the stands, waving. We wave back and he grins around his mouth guard, then gets back into the game.

I know some basics about football, but Landon takes the time to explain the details to me. With the two of them on my sides, no one says boo to me for the rest of the afternoon, and we have a good time watching the game. I try to take it all in: the band, the cheerleaders, the opposing team on the opposite side of the field, their band trying to be louder than ours. There's a festive air of excitement that seems to sink into my skin and swim around in my blood, revving my anticipation of each play.

Fortunately we win, and the other team trudges

from the field with their heads low as their fans file from the stands back to the parking lot. Landon, Milo and I wait for the stands to clear before we follow the line back to the concession area, then wait outside the locker room. When Jared emerges, he spots us right away and bounds over with a bright grin under his blue SFW ball cap.

"Congrats, man! You did great!" Landon greets him with a high five and they do that man-hug thing where they sort of bump chests but don't actually hug.

"Great game," Milo adds more mildly, with a pat on the back.

Jared's eyes turn to me expectantly and his expression suddenly turns nervous.

"Amazing," I agree with a smile, and his face relaxes. "And thanks for letting me wear your jersey. It pissed Amber off, so that's a win in my book."

Jared's head tips back and he lets out a deep, throaty laugh. "Well, I'll be. I suppose that did it indeed. But I should thank you for wearing it. I think it brought me luck," he adds with a wink.

My cheeks warm, and my gaze drops to the ground. That was definitely flirtatious.

"The team is going to Badger's to celebrate, you guys in?"

Landon agrees with enthusiasm and Milo mutters something about already having had Badger's today, but he agrees all the same.

"I dunno," I hedge. "I should probably text Roxanne

and make sure it's okay. They might already have started dinner at the house."

"I have an even better idea." Jared whips out his phone and sends off a text, then gets an immediate reply. "Cool. We're coming to your house for dinner. Sound good?"

"What?" I sputter. "I mean, sure, that sounds good to me, I just-"

"Don't worry about it. I told you Roxanne's my auntie, and judging from what Milo told me last weekend, you should already be aware we know our way around that kitchen," he adds with a wink.

"Yeah, you're right. I guess I keep thinking of town and Harridan House as two separate things. It's so remote from here, and school."

"It is, but we all have family who work there. Most of the town does. And they have parties and stuff for the holidays. We've spent a lot of time there."

The idea pops into my head before I even realize it, and a grin spreads across my face. "Okay, then let's go have dinner. And maybe you guys want to hang out after?"

They all agree enthusiastically, and my smile widens.

Excellent.

Chapter Twelve

MILO

~

After dinner we're lounging in Lex's room and bullshitting, but I can tell she wants something. There's something she's holding back, something she wants to ask us, but she's biding her time.

As we all are.

We're swiftly running out of time to tell her, and even though we've been spending as much time together as possible, it doesn't seem to get any easier. It's only been a week.

Now that Lex is on pack territory, she's going to manifest at the next full moon. She's already overdue; everyone has their awakening the first full moon after they turn seventeen. I assume this is the reason we're already sensing each other's emotions; we ought to be linked by now.

But no one knows how it works, how any of it truly will work, since her mom never claimed her role as alpha all those years ago. By birth she's the progeny of the *progeny* of the alpha, and it always runs through the Harridan female line.

However, since her mother never became alpha and Dom was forced to assume the role, we don't actually know what will happen when she manifests. If Dom had a fated mate, the line might have switched. Without one, Layla seems destined to take over.

The first lunar eclipse following her eighteenth birthday is when she's due to become alpha. According to the almanac, that's just over three months from today.

The full moon is barely a week away.

And Lex still doesn't know about any of it.

The guilt has been eating me alive. Landon, Jared, and I have discussed how to tell her endlessly. The day after she started classes, Dom changed his order and charged *us* with telling her the truth. As her fated mates, it makes sense. Our very biology draws us together, encourages us to trust and connect with one another.

But as an eighteen-year-old who just met my fated mate a week ago, it feels like way too much responsibility to bear.

Still, it has to be done.

I stare blankly at my phone, pretending to read something while Landon feigns watching tv in order to give Jared Lex's full attention. His confidence around her has grown since she agreed to wear his jersey, and he's finally starting to act more like himself around her. Still a little reserved, but then we all are, a little. There are so many secrets to keep, we have to be cautious at all times.

Right now he's regaling her with his collection of dad jokes, and an involuntary grin curls my lip when she laughs delightedly at each one.

"Okay, okay: What did the Gingerbread Man put on his bed?" Jared's grin is a mile wide and ultra white against his dark complexion.

"I dunno," Lex answers with a giggle. "What did the Gingerbread Man put on his bed?"

"Cookie Sheets!"

Lex snorts another laugh. "Did you get that one from a cookie-themed Laffy Taffy?"

Jared told her that the reason he likes the candy so much is because he enjoyed the jokes as a kid. He always had one of them in his lunch growing up, and he used to write the cheesy jokes down in a notebook every day.

"Nah, that one I got from the internet."

Lex yawns and stretches, faking boredom, but I sense her underlying tension. "So, you guys said you've come here a lot, growing up?"

"Yep," Jared answers. "We all have close family who

work here or used to, and the whole town is kind of like one enormous family, anyway."

I work to stop myself from snorting. *Understatement of the year.*

"So you guys must know a lot more about this house than I do? I bet you've explored the whole place." She's getting closer to what she wants. Her pulse is picking up, I spot the vein in her delicate neck throbbing from here.

Landon turns from the tv to catch my eye, and when Jared hesitates, I take over.

"Yeah, a little," I answer with equal nonchalance. "It's hard to resist a game of hide and seek in a place like this as a kid. As I recall, we got into trouble more than once."

"Did you ever come into this room? Mr. Carson said it used to be my mother's."

"I can't say that we did, to be honest. We mostly kept to the common spaces for fear of getting caught by Mr. Carson."

Landon chuckles in agreement, and Jared nods. "We got the run of the place, within reason."

"Did you ever go into the attic?" Her tone is nonchalant, but I can feel the tension emanating from her like a tangible thing.

This is what she's desperate to know. My eyes dart from Jared to Landon, but I can't think of a reason to deny it; it seems harmless enough.

"Yes, I think we did once or twice," I answer carefully, watching her reaction.

There's no mistaking it; excitement and hope fill her eyes and she lights up like a kid on Christmas morning.

"Could you show me?"

"Why do you want to see the attic?" Of course, I want to give her anything she asks for, but the necessity of following the alpha order and concealing our nature until the time is right takes precedence.

"Because Mr. Carson told me this used to be my mom's suite, and they put all of her things in storage in the attic when they decorated it for me." Her eyes dart around the room between the three of us. "I feel like the woman I knew, the woman who raised me before she died, was a stranger. I didn't even know her real name until last year. I hoped that coming here I'd get some answers, but it feels like they're all avoiding the topic completely." Her gaze drops to the ground and her tone is softer, sadder, when she continues. "I just want to know more about who I am."

A fierce desire to comfort her rips at my heart. My father told me about the ecstasy of having, then the agony of losing his mate. How the animal within is ten times more powerful in emotion than I'd ever experienced before. I'd ignored him, certain he was being overly dramatic. But now I'm not so sure.

Jared and Landon's faces tell me they feel exactly the same. We know each other almost better than we know ourselves, and if Lex had grown up with us, we'd already be a powerful team.

But she doesn't know us well enough, not yet. And we have to be careful or risk a second rejection in as many generations. One was unheard of, but two would mean the end of our pack as we know it.

And the alpha already told us it's our responsibility to prevent it, at all costs.

I reply with my gentlest tone. "I'm sorry, Lex. I can't imagine how hard that is. We obviously didn't know your mother, but we have heard a little about her. I don't see why it would be a problem for us to show you the attic. It is your house, after all."

Despite the concerned looks of my friends, the way Lex's eyes light up again fills me with relief. We aren't even linked yet, and I'm already desperate to give her anything she wants.

The full moon can't come fast enough.

～

Layla

～

It takes every ounce of courage I have to ask, but I am swiftly rewarded with my first dose of hope since arriving at Harridan House. Now the boys and I, with Milo in the lead, are filing up the curving staircase to the very top floor where the old servants' quarters are.

It's not as if I couldn't find the attic myself—obviously it's going to be upstairs as far as I can go—but something within me needed to ask permission from someone, anyone, to poke around. And if these boys are as familiar with this house as they said, they clearly have permission to explore, so that must extend to me.

Truthfully, I really don't want to do it alone. Whether it's dread of what I'll find out, or just fear of an old creaky mansion, something within me craves the company of these three on this particular mission.

Even in the hidden areas, the home seems impeccably maintained. If I had expected peeling wallpaper and shredded curtains, I would be horribly disappointed. The top floor hallway has neat carpet and freshly painted trim, with tastefully patterned paper lining the walls. The guys assure me that no one lives up here anymore. With only a dozen full-time staff, the decision was made to give them rooms similar to mine, but outfitted for two to share a suite.

The hallway seems impossibly long, but eventually we reach the end with a door just like the dozen we've already passed. Milo, Landon, and Jared exchange a swift look, then Milo opens the door and climbs yet another flight of stairs. A few seconds later, light floods through the doorway from the other side, and Landon gestures for me to follow Milo.

As if we have finally found the forgotten places of the castle, these stairs are hardwood, painted white but obviously faded with age. They creak under foot, and my heart rate rises with the sudden awareness that this is a place I'm not meant to see. Even if it's just because the people who work here labor to keep me surrounded by luxury and would be horrified at the idea of me in the spidery attic, a wave a guilt courses through my stomach. In my heart of hearts, I know that if he wanted me here, Mr. Carson would have taken me himself the day I asked about it.

However, I shove it down and finish my climb. Landon follows me, and Jared closes the door behind us before ascending.

Of course, I shouldn't be surprised that it's not a haunted-looking jumble of refuse from years past. Instead, there are neat rows of shelves, featuring plastic bins and cardboard boxes all carefully labeled with their contents. The closest shelves contain seasonal items the household must use annually to decorate for holidays. We travel down the rows, hunting for artifacts of more significance. There are tons of interesting things on these shelves, from extra decor to badminton sets.

Finally, in the last row, Milo pauses in front of a humble grey plastic bin. I scurry up beside him eagerly, and read 'Lily' in elegant script on the label. Yanking it from the shelf, I pull off the lid and peer into my first glimpse of my mother's true identity.

It's like a time capsule of a teenage girl from twenty years ago. It seems Mr. Carson is an old softy, because he apparently threw nothing away. Posters of boy bands, tiny pewter knickknacks of animals and fairies sleeping on toadstools, even a few framed photos of my mom—we could practically be twins, Uncle Dom wasn't lying—being goofy with friends.

And while it's all interesting, none of it is really giving me the answers I'm looking for. My heart drops in my chest—I must have expected some kind of silver bullet, perhaps a diary or something else that would just tell me *who she was*, but I find nothing of significance.

"Are there any other boxes with her name?" I ask the others hopefully. They search the surrounding shelves, but turn up nothing.

"They probably donated all the things that might be useful to someone else," Landon offers gently. "This is just the stuff that's personal to her. Keepsakes."

"Yeah," I agree, fishing one of the framed photos out. It's covered in seashells, and the photo shows my mom at a beach with three boys. She's maybe thirteen, and all four of them have water guns. They're lined up, hip to hip, with their arms around each other, grinning happily in the late afternoon sun.

As I examine each of their faces, I realize they all look vaguely familiar. "Do you guys know the boys in this photo?" I ask my companions.

Once again, they exchange a look, and my intuition sparks again. "Okay, out with it. You know who they are, don't you?"

Milo, ever the spokesperson for the group, sighs. "Yes. When your mom ran away, it was an enormous deal to the town. You might say that they never got over it. We grew up hearing about it like some kind of urban legend, people speculating about where she went, and why. I'd say most of our generation are pretty tired of the story. You have to understand, most of the people here grow up together, and grow up close. Every one of your mom and dad's friends felt as if they'd lost a member of their own family. Some were really bitter about it. These two," he pointed, "were the closest people to your mom and dad. They were all... best friends. The one on the left is Amber's dad, Peter Jean-Yves, and the one on the right with the red hair? That's Elliot Westley. You've met his sons, the twins who are always with Amber."

"But what about the one in the middle with her?"

Milo gives me an odd look. "That's your dad, Lex."

I squint at the photo. "Are you sure? He doesn't look like him." The boy in the picture has sandy blonde hair, and my father's hair was dark brown. "I suppose it's an old photo and people change. But why are you so sure?"

"Every few years, a local paper does a story about it. Even though people were certain she ran away, they both went missing as teenagers and someone drums up the idea that something more nefarious happened. They use their senior high school photos, and it's definitely them."

He stoops to fish another framed photo from the bin. It's my mom and the same three boys, along with several other classmates. They're older, and this time I can see the resemblance of the man I knew as my father. His hair is still that sandy blonde color, but the face is more like the man I knew and the realization strikes me like a hammer: he dyed his hair to change his appearance. My mom had the same thick, wild hair I do, but she cut it short and wore it in a pixie cut, despite my many attempts to shame her into growing out her mane. It was all part of the concealment of their identities.

I take a few more moments to absorb it all. "So when you said people were upset, that they felt betrayed by their own family, you meant that about Amber's father and the other guy, Elliot, right?"

Milo nods. "Yes. I can only imagine what it was like for Amber and the Wesley twins growing up. We heard the story so much we could recite it in our sleep, and our parents weren't even that close to your mom and dad. It was a tremendous scandal for a small town."

"I just don't get it. You mean to tell me that teenagers in love never run off from this place?"

"It's not exactly that," Landon interjects. "It's more about the fact that she was Lilliana Harridan. People expected a lot of her. The Harridans have been a feature of this town since before they built it; she wasn't just any teenager in love. It's more like the equivalent of someone from the royal family in England just disappearing and never being heard from again. Well, except for the whole 'royalty' thing. But if you haven't figured it out, the Harridans are kind of like royalty here."

I snort. "That doesn't seem to have done me any favors with people like Amber."

Landon's eyes soften with understanding. "I'm sorry, that's not really your fault. But I think your mom running away kind of created a fracture in the town that didn't exist before. Most people here love and support the Harridan family for everything they've done and continue to do for the community. But there are some, like Amber's family, who feel differently."

"So that's why she hates me? Because I'm a Harridan?" Just when I thought I was so fortunate to find out who I really am, it looks more and more like a curse.

"Sort of," Jared answers. "Amber's family, and a few others, feel the level of deference the rest of the town gives your family is... undeserved."

"It's not really anything to be too concerned about," Milo jumps in with a pointed glance at the other two. "Just know that there are some feuds in every small town, and that hostility isn't all your fault. It's hard to change someone's mind about something they've been taught since birth."

"And that's what, that my family is crap because my mom ran away as a teenager? Who holds that kind of grudge?"

"It was more about Amber's dad, and how he felt about your mom," Landon answers gently. "It's pretty well known that he and Elliot Wesley were both... in love with her. And she chose your father instead of them. They never got over it. Imagine being the woman he married, and finding out he still pines for his high school love? Imagine being Amber, growing up in that environment? It's a whole mess, and I'm not trying to make excuses for her, but I just thought you should know there's another side to the story."

I glance down at the photo one more time. The guys huddle protectively around my teenage mom, isolating her even from the other kids in the group who were clearly friends. The smile on her face is forced. I can see that now. She holds a notebook in one hand, and the other, almost concealed by her billowy skirt, clutches my father's.

Is this why you ran away? I wonder. *To escape the unwanted love of your two best friends?*

Or is there even more to the story?

Chapter Thirteen

LAYLA

~

This time, I'm certain I scream myself awake.

I hear my own voice, feel the fire of exertion in my throat as I sit up, panting. Once again, I'm soaked with sweat. Once again, the house is eerie and quiet. I listen for less than a minute before I hear the baying of wolves outside.

Even though I throw back the covers and dart to the window, I don't see the animals on the property. It sounds as if they're right outside my window, but nothing moves in shadows below.

After stripping off my damp pajamas and pulling on a fresh pair, I grab a drink and head back to bed. It's almost become a ritual now: I wake, change, then contemplate the latest dream/nightmare while my heart rate slows.

This time I was once again a wolf, and my companions were clearly distinguishable as wolf-versions of Milo, Landon, and Jared. We were running with the pack, and the entire dream was saturated with a feeling of belonging. My heart felt whole and happy. There were a few wolves ahead, leading, and the rest of the pack stretched out behind us, following.

In an instant, the feeling of the dream went from contentment to fear. The leaders picked up speed and no matter how I tried, I couldn't keep up. My legs worked faster and faster, my lungs threatening to explode in my chest, and they still disappeared into the night.

When I slowed and gave up, I realized I'd lost my companions, as well as the rest of the pack. Wolf-Layla whined softly, spinning on her padded feet, searching for anyone else.

But now I was alone, lost in the dark. I sniffed at the ground, trying to figure out if I should continue forward to catch the leaders, or turn back to rejoin the pack I'd left behind. The growls hit my ears a split second before their faces appeared in the darkness. Three wolves, their eyes gleaming, appeared in the underbrush on one side of the trail. With a snarl, they leapt for me and I scarcely had time to scream before I woke.

It is so bizarre. The dreams are so vivid, and while I can justify the subject given the nightly wolf calls and mountainous setting, I just can't understand why I've never had a single dream like this before moving to Smoky Falls. Sure, I've had nightmares. As a kid, I had them all the time. After my parents died and I ended up in foster care, I rarely slept hard enough to dream.

So perhaps that's it, then. I am finally to a place where I sleep, deeply enough to dream, and now I just have to get used to dreaming again. I wish it wasn't always heart-pounding, creepy-forest wolf dreams, but perhaps I need to count myself lucky that along with a home, and family, and new friends, I've found myself able to dream again.

I settle back into my bed as drowsiness washes over me, and drop into a deep, restful sleep.

∼

Layla

∼

Since it's Sunday, I know my uncle will be around. I've seen him during the week for brief glimpses at a few breakfasts, but he was always on his phone, or with Roxanne going down a checklist... if he was there at all. As often as not, I eat dinner with one or more of the staff, since Uncle Dom always seems to run off to a meeting or event in town. I know he's the mayor, but it mystifies me he has so many things to attend in such a small place.

However, it's definitely fair to say I understand now why he couldn't stay with me in LA—he barely stays in this house as it is.

But Roxanne assures me he'll be here tonight. Despite last weekend, Sunday is apparently when he and all the household staff have a sort of family dinner, which I guess now includes me.

I know now that he's the only one that's going to give me answers. Whether it's because they fear his reprisal or for some other reason, no one will give me more than a few tidbits about my mom. The boys were the most forthcoming last night in the attic, but even they don't know enough to satisfy my curiosity.

My uncle grew up with her. He was there, so he definitely can tell me more, if not all of, the story.

And tonight I plan to get answers.

I plot my attack as I wander the lush grounds of Harridan House, soaking in the warm sunlight and earthy fragrances that surround me.

It isn't a complicated plan; I'm going to play nice at dinner, then corner him and get to the bottom of the mystery surrounding my mom's childhood and what led to her running away in the first place.

Because it makes little sense. This place is magnificent—why would someone ever leave? Yes, it's a little lonely in the giant castle. But she had parents and a sibling, and clearly she had friends. It's a cute small town with a hipster-wilderness vibe, and short of a shopping mall and a movie theater, Smoky Falls seems to have everything a person could want. I certainly understand why people *don't* leave this place; I've seen what the world offers and there's not a lot of good out there. Sure, a bigger city offers anonymity, and there are things to see in the world like the pyramids, the Statue of Liberty, the Eiffel Tower... all places to visit, then go home.

But nothing ever felt right the way Smoky Falls does. Even with my entire childhood spent growing up in LA, I never felt like I was home. My parents moved us constantly from one apartment to another. We never settled in one place for more than a year. Everything was temporary, and that was *before* I ended up in foster care.

Here, everything feels permanent, solid, trustworthy and inevitable. I've scarcely been here a week, and it's already the most *home* I've felt in my entire life. Despite my initial fears, and mean kids at school—seriously we're in college, you'd think they would have grown out of it?—I have no desire to leave.

But I need to know the truth. My mother never did anything that wasn't for a reason, and I know, deep in my heart, that she had her reasons for leaving Smoky Falls despite a lack of obvious ones.

My mind flashes briefly to Derrek and my street family, a slight pang in my chest for the people who were my entire world just a year ago. Now they seem like a distant past, almost so far removed as to be a dream more than a memory.

Something about this place is magical. Restorative. As a kid surviving on the street, I learned really quickly to box up fears or emotions of any kind. I didn't have the luxury of being afraid, or sad, or hurt. You'd think someone would need years of therapy to get over that, and to be fair, perhaps my year with Roxanne was a sort of deprogramming to help transition me to a more normal life.

But at the same time, I'm now perfectly comfortable pulling out those emotions, unboxing them, and examining them one by one. They don't bother me to consider as part of my distant past. Even the attack that I only remember in flashes is an unemotional memory. I healed, I recovered, and while I bear the scars on my arms and chest, I don't carry any ill effects in my heart. I wonder who attacked me, but I assume it had to have been random. There's no other explanation.

The only thing that continues to bother me is the mystery of why my parents left in the first place. Why drag me through all of those roach-infested apartments, barely surviving, when I could have grown up here in a literal *palace*?

The urge to let it go is strong—after all, I'm here now. What else matters?—but the need for answers is stronger.

Tonight I'll go to dinner, be the perfectly behaved niece, and then I'll corner my uncle and finally get some answers.

Chapter Fourteen

LAYLA

~

So this is what a normal family dinner looks like.

Seated in the 'breakfast room' with my uncle, most of the staff, and Roxanne, it's difficult to describe the odd formality of the occasion when it's outwardly supposed to be casual.

The staff who are not working—I guess this alternates by weeks, so everyone gets to join 'family dinner'—are wearing normal clothes, not uniforms like they do through the day. Food is served 'family style' with the platters passed around while everyone chatters. There's light conversation, background music, and an outward sense of ease.

And yet, the tension is thick among the party. The staff speak in low tones to each other, and Mr. Carson sits beside Uncle Dom, chatting as they eat. However, it's not the same lighthearted conversation I overheard when I slipped into the kitchen last week and observed them enjoying their meal without my uncle's supervision.

I'm at my uncle's left, and I'm trying—but failing—to come up with conversation.

He asks about my first week of school, the football game, and how things are going with the guys, which I answer as conversationally as I can. But when I turn the conversation to him and his work, his replies are curt and he quickly reengages Mr. Carson in conversation about household matters.

Now I'm just picking at my asparagus, attempting to come up with something more engaging to talk about.

"Is there something wrong with the food?" Roxanne eyes me as she sips from her wineglass, her eyebrow raised knowingly.

"No, the food is fine," I sigh. Leaning closer to her, I add in a lower voice, "I was just hoping to talk more to Uncle Dom, and he doesn't seem interested in what I have to say."

Roxanne observes Dom on my right for a moment, then nods. "Yes, this is usually his chance to catch up with the concerns of the household with less... formality. Even though they work for him, he wants to make sure everyone here feels important."

"So, when do I get the chance? He's barely spoken a

dozen words to me since the first night I arrived." I know I sound pouty, but I can't help it.

Roxanne's dark eyes reflect the flickering candlelight from the table decor. "Dominic usually spends a few hours in the library on Sunday nights. Perhaps, after dinner, that would be a good place for you to talk. Maybe you can get to know each other better."

I accept her suggestion with a nod and return my focus to my food.

This may be my first strike, but even in baseball, I'd have two more to go.

And now I have all the time in the world to get answers.

~

Layla

~

After dinner, I return to my room and change into sweats before making my way to the library. I shouldn't be surprised, but there's already a roaring fire going, with a decanter, glass, and bucket of ice on a tray positioned on the coffee table.

Oh yeah, Dom definitely has a routine.

Figuring he has a favorite spot as designated by the refreshments, I choose a random book and settle into a chair that's tucked in a cozy nook. There's a partial shelf of books between me and the rest of the room, and my chair faces the window with a view over the dark gardens behind the house. I settle back into the chair, tug a fuzzy throw blanket over my lap, and crack open my book. I'm determined to wait as long as it takes for him to show.

It turns out the crime thriller I picked up is actually engrossing, and it takes a while before I realize I'm no longer alone in the room.

I sense something, and when I glance up, he's standing with his back to me, one hand on the mantle of the fireplace, and the other supporting his forehead. I set the book in my lap and prepare to speak, but something stops me and I take a moment to observe him instead.

He's pulled a heavy cardigan over the shirt and dress pants he wore at dinner, and seeing him in this moment feels... obtrusive. Like this is a peek behind the curtain, something I'm not supposed to see, something no one is supposed to see. His very aura feels tired, like the weight of the world is dragging him down.

Suddenly self-conscious, I'm not sure if I should announce myself or just shrink back in my chair and hope he doesn't notice me. But Roxanne told me he'd be here, that it would be a good time for us to talk, so it can't be wrong for me to intrude.

While my mind flits back and forth between resolving to hide out for a while or announcing myself and demanding his attention, fate intervenes on my behalf.

The book slips from my lap and lands on the hardwood floor with a slap.

My uncle doesn't jump. Instead, he whips around and crouches slightly, a silvery glow of reflected light in his eyes as they scan my corner.

"Sorry." I stand and retrieve the book. "I didn't mean to startle you. I was just reading."

Straightening immediately, an indulgent smile crosses his face. "It's not a problem, Layla. Why don't you come join me by the fire? The light's better here, and it's a good deal warmer."

My window nook is actually chilly, and it seems I might get the opportunity I hoped for. Heart leaping, I replace the blanket on the chair and move to a spot on the couch.

"Actually, I was hoping to have time to talk to you," I start cautiously. "Roxanne said you usually give the staff your attention during dinner, but you'd be here after."

Uncle Dom chuckles and takes a seat. "She did, huh? It's true, I suppose. I'm sure you've seen by now I get little time to myself. There are a lot of duties that I... as mayor... have to attend to. Way more than I realized before I had the job," he adds with a snort. "But that doesn't mean I don't have time for you at all. I'm sorry we haven't had much time to speak."

"That's okay, I understand. It seems to keep you pretty busy."

"It does," he agrees.

"Are you going to run again?"

His eyes flash to me in confusion. "Run again?"

"For mayor. You serve for a term, like a president or a governor, right?"

"Oh, right. No, I don't think I will run again. After this term is up, I think I'll be happy to step down from public service."

"Well, that's good that you tried it, right? And now you can do something else, maybe something you're more passionate about, and someone new can take over."

"Yes, exactly." His eyes drift to the fire. "I think it's time for someone new to take over."

Desperate not to lose his attention now that I have it, I rush to throw out a new topic. "Uncle Dom, would you tell me about my mom?"

His gaze whips back to me. "What do you want to know?"

"Anything," I reply honestly. "I feel like the woman I knew until the day she died was a fabrication, a myth. You're her brother. You clearly knew her better than anyone."

He settles back in his seat with a thoughtful expression. "Yes, I suppose it would seem so. But let me ask you first: What was she like before she died? I haven't seen her since she was seventeen. I always wondered what she was like as an adult. As a mother."

I dredge up the memories of life before foster care and the streets. "She was strict, but loving. I had a lot of rules growing up, but we lived in a lot of crappy neighborhoods, so I knew it was for my protection. She and my dad were affectionate with me and with each other. I always felt loved and cared for, not like a lot of my friends whose parents were never around. There was always someone home, always someone waiting for me. We always had dinner together if my dad wasn't working a late shift. They were funny together. Dad always lightened her up. He could make her laugh, no matter how mad she was. When he wasn't there, she was much quieter. She never talked about herself, or where she grew up.

"Which is why I was so surprised to find out *this* is where she grew up. I thought she had a rough life, maybe abusive parents. She basically implied that she had a terrible childhood, and she wanted to spare me the details. Which is why I want to know what her life here was actually like, since she clearly didn't have the unfortunate upbringing I imagined."

Uncle Dom sighs. "Thank you for sharing that. It pains me to hear she was quiet without Brandon—that was your father's real name. They loved each other, of course, but your mom was always the life of the party, always outgoing, always happy. Well, until about a year before she ran away. But before that, she was like a light no one could extinguish.

"She didn't have a dark or abusive childhood, at least to my knowledge. Our parents were loving and attentive, and we clearly didn't lack for anything.

"But she was the eldest, and there were a lot of expectations about how she would live her life. I think that was probably the biggest part of what drove her away. Our mother had very high expectations for Lilliana. Nothing was ever good enough. And I think knowing they laid her entire life out for her is what drove her to run away.

"She wanted freedom, and our mother would not let her have it. Honestly, it shouldn't have been such a surprise, but perhaps we didn't really know her as well as we thought. I know I, like my parents, knew she was unhappy, but just assumed she would grow up and face her responsibilities head on.

Instead, the day before her seventeenth birthday she disappeared with Brandon and we never heard from her again."

I listen with rapt attention as he relays the story. Sighing, he leans forward to fix himself a drink, and I ask the next question on my mind. "What about my grandparents?'

Dom's eyes track back to me from his glass, and he smiles sadly. "My mom, your grandma, would have been so happy to know you. You really look just like Lilliana."

"Thank you, but what I mean is, what were they like?"

"Oh, well, they were wonderful parents. They had high expectations, but I think that's inevitable with a family like ours. They spent vast resources trying to find Lilliana, but she covered her tracks too well. Of course, they were devastated, but eventually they had to make new plans. They put their focus on making me their heir, and all the responsibilities my sister ran away from landed on me."

"And how do you feel about that?" I wonder aloud. "Do you resent her for leaving?"

"Resent her?" shock crosses his face. "No, of course not. I understand why she did it. Well, maybe at first I resented her a little, because I was just a kid and suddenly my world changed. But as I got older, I realized I understood her motivation better, and I didn't hold it against her."

"That's pretty generous of you, considering it sounds like she just shirked her family expectations and left you holding the pieces."

Dom sighs again and takes a slow sip. "To be honest with you, Layla, it hasn't been easy. And I'm tired. It's way more than I can handle, and I'm really not cut out for this job. But I'm glad you're here. It was even worse, knowing I didn't have anyone to hand all of this down to. Now there's someone to take over once I'm gone, and it is a relief."

"Didn't you ever want a family of your own?"

"I did, but my responsibilities here made it impossible for me to get out and find someone."

"Surely you could find lots of women who'd love to live in a castle and be waited on hand and foot," I snort. "Did you try a dating app?"

Dom answers with a snort of his own. "I'm afraid it's not that simple, but I would have if I could. Regardless, you're here now and that solves most of my problems. But it's a lot of responsibility." He eyes me speculatively. "Do you think you're up for it?"

"Truthfully, Uncle Dom, I feel more at home here than anywhere else I've lived in my life. I'm just so grateful to have a family, to have a home, and a place that I belong. I'm happy to help and take it over one day."

He sighs in relief. "Thank you, Layla. That's exactly what I needed to hear."

Chapter Fifteen

LAYLA

~

Even though I sleep heavily with the satisfaction of finally getting some answers from my uncle, it doesn't keep the dreams at bay.

Once again, I wake from a frightening dream featuring wolves, to the howls of the same creature somewhere nearby in the forest.

After my new nightly ritual of changing pajamas and switching sides of the bed, I settle in uneasily.

The dream was different this time, as if my subconscious took the information from my chat with Dom and added another layer. Now I know the wolves ahead of me, the leaders, were Dom, my mom, and dad. They raced ahead, left me behind even as I sped to keep up, losing the Milo, Landon, and Jared wolves in my haste.

And just like last night, three wolves jumped from the shadows and attacked me.

While the dreams were odd at first, they now give me a terrible sense of foreboding.

The feeling of abandonment by my parents makes sense. But Dom is *here*. He took me in and is caring for me. Maybe I'm just fearful he'll leave me, like my parents did?

And Jared, Milo, and Landon seem pretty capable of keeping up with me. There hasn't been a moment I wasn't either here, under the protection of my uncle, or with one or more of them. Have I already grown so attached I'm afraid to lose them, too? I like them, but it's only been a week.

Of course, the part about being attacked by a literal pack of wolves makes sense, and I don't need to be a dream guru to figure that one out. New place, people who seem to hate me for no fault of my own... that's pretty easy to interpret.

A quick glance at my phone tells me it's after midnight—too late to text Milo, I'm sure. Even if he was up, it would come across rather stalkerish to just start messaging him in the middle of the night.

Yawning, I set my phone aside and settle back into my pillows. Maybe all the dreams will make more sense tomorrow, after my subconscious has time to pick them all apart.

Jared

"We have to tell her, man." Milo is riding with me to school today, and I need to get this off my chest. "The longer we drag it out, the harder it will be."

"I know, but come on. How do you just tell someone they're about to sprout fur and bay at the moon? We grew up knowing this was the truth. Lex knows nothing about it."

"Why do you call her that, anyway? I thought her name was Layla?" My eyes dart from the road to Milo, stretched out in the passenger seat of my pickup.

"She said it the first day we met her. It must be a nickname she used in LA, but she hasn't told that name to anyone else, so now it's stuck in my mind and it feels like something special." He shrugs. "It's what she wanted me to call her, so I'm gonna use it until she says something different. Also, technically her name is Lilliana, like every alpha Harridan. Whether she knows it or not."

"That's still weird to me."

"Guys do it all the time. Name their kid after themselves. You want to talk about spooky, think about the fact that every first-born kid in the Harridan line has been a girl for at least two centuries. Maybe more. We just don't get all the details."

"You're right, that's weirder."

"No, what's weird is you deciding to come in early

to campus when you don't have Monday classes. What are you doing, anyway?"

I shift in my seat. "I felt like I missed out, not meeting Layla at the same time as you guys. So I thought it would help for me to spend more time with her, like before classes and stuff. I didn't do my reading this weekend, so I was just planning on hitting the library while you guys are in class."

"So this is all about a few minutes before class that you missed out on?" Milo's dark eyebrow rises, and he stares at me with obvious disbelief.

"Well, not exactly." Turning the wheel, I pull into the Painted Moose. "Layla mentioned she likes vanilla lattes, so I thought I'd pick her up one. You want anything?"

A laugh bursts from Milo's lips. "Jared, I didn't know you had it in you, you big softie. You got out of bed hours before you had to just so you could bring her a coffee? You're already smitten, my friend."

I join the queue for the drive-through, glad my dark cheeks don't show the blush I feel heating them. "Well she is our fated, and the alpha charged us with making her feel at home. Part of that is growing her attachment to us and this place. I figured a coffee couldn't hurt."

When I pull up to the window and place my order, Milo leans over and requests a flat white. "Should we get Landon anything?"

"Nah, you know he prefers those nasty energy drinks to coffee. That's it, thanks!"

We pay the girl, then pull ahead to the pick-up

window. Once we have our drinks and are on our way toward Smoky Falls College, I bring it up again.

"So, when are we gonna tell her?" I lift my cup of basic brew and blow across the tiny hole in the lid, praying the drink won't scald my tongue when I take a sip.

Milo's answer nearly makes me spill the drink entirely. "Tonight."

"Tonight?!" I sputter, setting my cup in the cupholder to avoid injury.

"Yeah, tonight. Weren't you just saying we needed to tell her?" Milo removes the lid from his coffee and sucks the foam from the top casually.

I grimace, then try to drive as carefully as possible. I do not want to end up cleaning milky coffee out of my truck.

"Yeah, but I was meaning we needed to come up with a plan. We've got a week before she has to manifest."

"Five days, actually. It's this Friday."

"Shit. For some reason, that feels ten times worse." Craving caffeine, I'm tempted to grab my coffee while I steer one-handed, but Milo's is still wide open and I choose to focus on driving instead.

"I know. That's why we need to tell her tonight."

"And how exactly do you plan to do that? I don't think they make 'surprise, you're a wolf!' balloons."

Milo finishes adding sugar and replaces the cap on his drink. "I was thinking we'd show her."

"*Show* her? Are you absolutely out of your mind?"

Distracted, I had started to drift into the other lane and I correct savagely, jostling Milo who holds his cup aloft but fortunately doesn't spill.

"Dude, take it easy. I don't need third-degree burns today!"

"What do you mean, *show* her?" I growl, my eyes darting between his face and the road.

"I mean that instead of going to run with the alpha tonight, we tell Layla to meet us outside and *show* her. It's not like she's just going to believe it if we tell her."

"Why not?" I argue. "She seems pretty cool to me. She might be more open-minded than you think."

"Once again, you're thinking like someone who has known about shifters since you were born. This is all new to her. As far as she's concerned, the paranormal is all fantasy. She's going to think we're crazy or lying if we just tell her."

"Fine. So how do you see this playing out?" I turn into the parking lot at SFC, easing into a spot.

"Let's just get through the day," Milo suggests, grabbing his bag and hopping out without spilling a drop of coffee in my truck. "We'll plant the seeds before we leave for the day, and I'll get her outside tonight. Just… do your best to be charming, okay?"

After shouldering my bag, I hold up Layla's coffee in mock salute. "Aye aye, captain."

Layla

~

"That's so thoughtful, thank you!" I accept the coffee from a beaming Jared, and Milo leans against the wall with a crooked grin and sips his own drink. "But did you get anything for Landon?"

"Nah, they know I only drink these." He holds up a brightly colored energy drink can and takes a long swig.

Milo pulls a face. "You know those are full of chemicals, right?"

"Yeah, and you know everything in the world is made up of chemicals, just in different forms, right? So what does it matter if it's what I like?"

"Whatever." Clearly, they've had this conversation a lot.

My brain finally catches up to the fact that it's odd for Jared to be here. "Jared, I thought you don't have morning classes on Mondays?"

He smiles sheepishly. "I didn't do any of my homework over the weekend, and I figured I could use the study time in the library. Milo lives next door to me and it's out of the way for Landon to pick him up, so it all works out. Plus, Painted Moose is worth getting up for."

"Well, I appreciate it, thank you." I take a sip, closing my eyes and making an appreciative sound as the warm liquid hits my tongue and I taste a perfect vanilla latte.

When I open my eyes, I realize all three guys are

staring at me, glassy-eyed.

"What?"

They startle as if they'd been in a trance. "Nothing," Milo says smoothly. "Is it how you like?"

"Yes, actually. I'm impressed you knew," my eyes drift to Jared. "I don't remember mentioning it."

"You did, Saturday night," he rushes to explain. "You said Milo and Landon took you to the Painted Moose and you had an iced mocha because Milo recommended it, but you prefer vanilla lattes and wanted to try one next time. So, here you go, next time." He recites the interaction as if he'd memorized it by heart. It was clearly important to him and I don't remember at all, but the thought behind it flames my cheeks once more.

"Well, thank you again. It's perfect. No offense, Milo, but I think the other was too sweet for me."

"Hey, only the strong survive," he winks. "Shall we get to class?"

With promises to meet Jared for lunch, we head to American History class, and take our seats with me in the middle, just like last week.

The day has already begun to feel routine as we make our way through classes. The guys swap out, so I'm never alone. Savannah and a few others sit with us at lunch, and she apologizes for not being at the game Saturday as if I were expecting her to be. I tell her it's totally fine, but she promises to sit with me for the next home game in a few weeks.

By the time classes are over for the day, I'm already dreading the pile of homework I need to complete. I'd much rather curl up with a mystery book in the library instead of taking notes on five chapters of pre-civil war American History to prepare for a test at the end of the week.

As if he read my mind, Milo asks, "Hey Lex, would you like to study together tonight?"

"That would be great, but I'd have to ask-"

"It's no biggie, we can come up to Harridan House. I bet we can even get Susan to pull out those cookies."

Jared gives Milo an odd look. "I'd love to, but I have practice for the next couple of hours."

"Oh, sorry, I meant later. After dinner. Can you come then?"

Jared nods slowly. "Yeah, that would work. Landon, do you want me to pick you up? I'm assuming I'm already driving Milo, anyway."

"Sure, sounds good to me." Landon grins, turning his rock-star smile on me. "Any excuse to hang out with Layla some more? I'm game. Bonus if we actually get homework done."

A kernel of panic rises in my chest. "Guys, this all sounds like fun, but I really should check with my uncle-"

"It's already done," Jared puts away his phone. "I texted my auntie, and she said it's fine. I'm telling you, we're always in and out of that house anyway, and it's your home, too. Maybe you should talk to Dom if it makes you uncomfortable. I'm sure he'd say you're welcome to have guests whenever you want. We've all been given a standing invitation to come over whenever."

"You have?" I search their faces, each one nodding seriously. "Huh. Okay. Then I guess I'll stop freaking out. I'm sorry, I just… am not used to this yet, I guess." That is an understatement. At the foster home, they strictly forbade us from bringing friends over, and before that, my mom was extremely wary of guests. I could only think of a handful of times I'd seen someone other than myself or my parents in any of our apartments.

"No worries." Milo's signature half-smile slides into place. "We'll text you when we're on our way. Sound good?"

"Yeah, perfect," I return his smile. Now I can spend the next couple hours reading whatever I want with complete ease, knowing they'd be turning up later to study.

We say our goodbyes and I meet Maxwell out front, already calculating how many chapters of my novel I can get in before dinner.

Chapter Sixteen

LAYLA

~

Studying with the guys is fun, if a little distracting. Milo manages to sweet talk Susan into cookies and hot chocolate after dinner, and we post up in my suite reading quietly, with the occasional joke or exclamation as someone checks their phone and reports the latest social media drama.

Since I've never really had social media, I don't get what the fuss is about. My mom didn't allow me to create profiles *anywhere*—of course, now I know why—and living on the street I didn't have regular access to the internet so I just never bothered.

Now I live in a small town and have a smart phone, but only really know like ten people and I have their phone numbers, so the appeal is still lost on me. Each of the guys is trying to convince me to join their favorite, and it's kind of amusing to watch them argue.

"You have to go with the classic," Milo states. "Instagram is just photos and reels, and you can follow celebrities you like, look at pictures from travel bloggers, find recipes... it's a lot less bullshit than other sites."

"Snap is photos too, and you can do all of that plus send direct photos and messages that automatically erase," Landon argues, turning his gaze to me with pink cheeks. "I mean, in case you want to share something with one person, but you don't want them to keep it. Plus, you get points, so it's like a game."

Jared shakes his head. "No, TikTok is the best because it has the funniest content. People do pranks, make joke videos, or share funny stuff. Plus, you can do viral dance challenges or just share videos of cats. It's pretty much whatever you want."

I can't help laughing at all of them, earnestly trying to persuade me to use their preferred app. "What's wrong with actual text messaging? I can send you guys photos, videos, and messages directly. You can share anything you want me to see. Why do we need to do it someplace else?"

"Well, in order for me to share a TikTok with you, you'd have to have the app to watch it," Jared shrugs, "but I see your point. If it's just you and me, I don't need anything else."

"I'm sure I'll check them out at some point, but I've still got a lot on my plate for now."

The guys nod as if they understand, and the room becomes quiet once more. I go back to my reading, but a few minutes later, Milo clears his throat.

"Hey Lex?"

I look up and take in his nervous expression. "Yeah?"

"You remember the first day we met, when you said you found wolf prints in the dirt?"

Landon and Jared exchange a look, then refocus on me.

"Yeah?"

"Well, I did some research—because it seemed so strange—and it turns out there actually are wolves around here."

Vindication rises in my chest. "I *knew* I wasn't crazy. I swear I hear them every night, but everyone acts like I'm making it up. I told a few people the first time, but they said it must have been in my dream."

"You dream about wolves?" Landon asks. At the same time Jared inquires, "You hear the wolves at night?"

Heat rushes to my cheeks. "Yeah. Ever since I arrived here, I've had strange, super-realistic dreams about wolves. I wake up every night, just after midnight, and I can hear them howling. It sounds like they're so close, but I can't see them from the windows."

"Have you ever gone outside to get a better look?" Milo's voice is measured.

"No... Uncle Dom made me promise I'd never go

into the woods alone. And to be honest, it's kind of creepy, waking up like that. It feels like the entire house is empty at night."

"Well, what if we do it together?"

"Do what together?" My eyes narrow, and I watch him carefully.

"What if we—the four of us—hang out until midnight, then go check it out?"

His offer pulls me up short. "You would do that?"

Landon looks at Milo with a peculiar expression. "Yeah, are you sure about that? Seems like a bad idea."

"Yeah, I'm sure. I think it's time we got to the bottom of this, don't you?" Even though I can sense another meaning, an implied intent, behind his words, I can't fathom what it would be.

"If Layla's in, I'm in," Landon shrugs. "I've always been more of a night owl, anyway."

"I dunno about the night owl part, but I'm in," Jared agrees. "Layla?"

Even though I'm thrilled at the idea of finally seeing the wolves I've been hearing every night, my pulse races with fear. Is this a good idea? I've always trusted my instincts and they've been screaming at me to run out into the forest at midnight, despite my uncle's warning. With these guys at my side I wouldn't be alone, and I wouldn't be afraid.

A snippet of my dream returns to me just then, causing my heart to leap to my throat: me as a wolf, running ahead, and leaving the wolf guys behind. The darkness, the attack by other wolves.

Well, I will just have to make sure not to morph into a wolf or run off, I think to myself dryly.

When I speak, my voice is firm. "Yeah, I'm in."

∼

Layla

∼

The guys text their families, letting them know they're staying late at my house, and we go back to studying. At first I think it's super cool of their parents to not care… then I realize we're all technically adults. Despite the many ways my years on the streets instantly aged me, there are some things about me that are apparently severely stunted. Now that I live in a house with a family again—sort of—I'm right back to a fourteen-year-old girl, believing I'll be told no when I ask to do anything, and have a curfew before the sun goes down.

Of course, I understand why my mom did a lot of those things, now. Roxanne never really pushed a curfew in LA, aside from forbidding me to go to North Hollywood again. But I also never asked to go out or stay out late. I wasn't in school making friends and I had little interest in meeting people online, so I just focused on my rehab and prep work for the GED, and that was pretty much it.

Now I still have to remind myself that I'm an adult and can do whatever I want.

Like having three hot boys in my room past midnight. Even the thought of it makes my heart race, let alone the idea that it's *these* three boys. Darkly sexy Milo, gorgeous but shy Landon, and all-American football-playing Jared.

No one comes to check on us, or suggest that it's long past time the boys should go home. As the hours pass, I settle in to the idea that we're doing nothing wrong.

My eyelids start growing heavy, and I allow them to droop for longer periods of time.

As if reading my mind, Milo yawns and glances at his watch. "I think I'm tapped out on the studying, guys. Why don't we watch a movie or something?"

Landon and Jared agree, stretching, and offer to run downstairs and raid the kitchen. Despite the well-stocked cupboard in my closet, they are insistent on stealing some of Susan's cookies.

Milo and I rearrange the furniture, moving aside the coffee table at his insistence. "Landon will want to sit on the floor, I promise," he winks, then gestures to the couch. "Which spot do you want?"

"Um, it doesn't really matter," I hedge, suddenly nervous. He's standing so close his warm fragrance fills my nose, and in the absence of the other two, it's suddenly dead-silent in my sitting room. I can hear my own heart pounding.

"Well, I always prefer to have an armrest, so I'd probably pick that corner," he points.

"Okay, that makes sense." As if I'd given him permission, he sits.

"You should sit next to me," He murmurs, tapping the cushion beside him. His voice is a soft caress, a gentle request that sends heat pooling in my belly.

"What if I want an arm rest?" I tease breathlessly.

"You can lean on me."

Trying to slow my racing heart, I claim the middle cushion and tug my leg underneath me. I'm astutely aware of the heat rolling off Milo's body mere inches away, and it's making me nervous.

In an effort to avoid his gaze and thin the tension in the air, I reach for the remote. "What should we watch?"

Milo doesn't answer me right away, and when I glance to my left to see if he's distracted I find him millimeters from my face, his hooded eyes intense as they stare back at me.

Electricity crackles in the air between us, my every nerve seemingly alight with it. The hairs on my arms rise, and I'm entirely trapped in his gaze.

Milo's eyes are locked on mine, his pupils so wide they almost swallow the bright sapphire-blue color. He reaches up slowly as if to tuck a strand of hair behind my ear, and I wait, breathless, to feel the light stroke of his fingertip.

Instead, I'm completely shocked when he grabs the back of my neck and pulls me closer, his mouth catching mine roughly.

A low moan escapes my lips and I melt into him, the

fire of his kisses peppered with the electric tingles I've come to associate pleasantly with all three of these boys. My hands rise to grip his shirt, pulling him closer before I run my fingers down the hard planes of his chest. Amusement flickers at the back of my mind when I feel his stomach flutter lightly under my touch.

Clearly, he's not as cool as he acts, because he sure seems just as excited as I am.

His cedar and sunshine fragrance surrounds me, and he tastes like the peppermint he had just a few moments before. I feel as if I'm about to burst out of my skin; it's too much and not enough all at the same time. I want to feel his bare skin under my palms at the same time I question if this is a good idea at all, given the two other guys and their super close friendship.

Confused, I pull back, gasping, and Milo releases his grip on my neck. He's equally out of breath, but his eyes are still hungry despite the concern I can read all over his expression.

"Lex, I'm-"

"No, it's okay. I'm not upset," I rush to reassure him, threading my fingers through his and enjoying the residual tingles. "I'm just a little surprised, and the others will be back any minute. We haven't really talked about... this." I gesture between us wordlessly. "Given how close you guys all are, I don't want there to be any drama."

Milo snorts and runs his free hand through his tousled hair. "Yeah, I know what you mean. But Lex?"

His eyes change from relief to smoulder in a nanosecond.

"Yes?" I reply, breathless, clenching my thighs in a desperate reminder to myself to behave.

"I've been waiting to do that since the greenhouse," he whispers, leaning in to press a tender kiss to my cheek, followed by another under my ear, then my jaw. Sighing, he leans back. "It was even better than I imagined." He treats me to his one-sided, sexy smirk that makes the butterflies dance in my belly.

If I wasn't a puddle before, I most certainly I am now. "Me too," I return his grin.

Landon and Jared choose that moment to stomp through the open doorway. "We have returned from our triumphant excursion!" Jared grins, holding up the coveted cookie tin.

As if sensing the charge in the atmosphere, Landon glances at us curiously, his gaze traveling from our clutched fingers to our flustered expressions. A small smile curls his lips, but he says nothing, depositing a pile of food directly in my lap and seating himself at my feet.

Jared claims the spot to my right, and it takes a few moments, but we manage to choose something to watch together without too much bickering.

Heat floods my cheeks as I try—and fail—*not* to think about kissing Milo during the movie. I make a genuine effort to pay attention, but it's all a jumble of colors and shapes moving on a distant screen. Meanwhile, I'm hyper-aware of Milo's body next to mine, the warmth from his skin, his palm pressed to my palm while his fingers lightly graze the back of my hand.

If Jared spotted us holding hands, he didn't react, and Landon didn't seem upset or surprised by the development. So I suppose that means he's fine with it. A tiny pang squeezes in my chest—I sort of thought I had a mutual attraction with Landon, too—but Milo feels right.

In fact, they all feel right. Landon rests his head against my crossed legs, and Milo and Jared's hips press against mine. But rather than feeling crowded, I feel... comforted. The tingles from the contact with these three boys notwithstanding.

Time passes quickly, and before I know it, Milo is hitting pause on the TV. "It's almost midnight. Are you guys ready?" His serious gaze travels to Landon, then to Jared, and finally to me.

The other guys look extremely nervous, which surprises me. I try to reassure them. "Come on guys, it's just some wolves. I'm sure with so many of us, we have nothing to worry about. Let's do this!"

When we emerge from my suite, the hallway lights are all off, but with four cellphone flashlights, we see passably well. As if by telepathy, we all head toward the stairs instead of the tiny elevator, and even my clumsy footsteps are quiet as we descend the curving staircase.

We reach the bottom and I head toward the front door, but Milo stops me with a gentle hand on my shoulder. "No, let's use the back door," he says softly. "This way."

I follow him through the kitchen to the rear entrance, and when I check the time on my phone, it says 11:59. My heart rate has grown steadily since we left my room, and now it's positively racing.

There's energy in the air, like static electricity. I can feel it on my skin, the same way the close proximity to these boys feels. I glance between their faces, and they all look nervous, practically sick to their stomachs. *Funny, that's sort of how I feel.*

"Are you guys okay? If you're that worried about it, we don't have to go out," I offer quickly. "I appreciate you being willing to check things out with me, but you look completely freaked."

"It's not that," Milo says in a shaky voice. "Lex, we have to tell you something."

"Now? Can't it wait until after we see the wolves?"

He shakes his head, dark eyes gleaming in the low light pouring through the windows. "No, it can't. Because..." the words pour from his lips in a rush of air, "because we *are* the wolves."

I snort a laugh. "Haha, very funny. You'll have to try better than that."

"No, he's being serious, Layla." Landon's lips are in a tight, hard line, and his face ghostly pale.

"There's a lot you don't know about this place, girl," Jared adds. "We don't have much time to explain, but Dom charged us with telling you before Friday, so here goes."

"Dom did what? Wait, is this some kind of prank?" My jaw clenches and I glare at all three of them, arms crossed. "Whatever this is, it's not funny."

"It's not a prank, Layla. It's the truth. You feel different here, right? Here in this place, in this house, in Smoky Falls, and with us?"

His words stop the angry retort on my tongue. It is almost word for word what I've been thinking. "Yes," I reply slowly. "But that's just because I've never had a home like this, or lived in a place like Smoky Falls."

Milo snorts. "Well, that certainly is true. You've never lived in a place like Smoky Falls. But it's more than that. You can feel it, deep beneath your skin. Maybe you didn't know how to put words to it, how to understand it, but you *know* something is just different. Here, and with us. I know you feel something about us, Lex."

"And how are you so sure?" I challenge for the sake of being difficult. I know *exactly* what he means.

"Because we can feel it, too. We feel when you're nervous or scared, angry or happy. We can feel when you're keeping something from us. Look, I don't have a lot of time to explain everything, but I figured this was the simplest way to get you to believe what we're trying to tell you."

"And that is what, that you're the wolves leaving paw prints in the garden?" My eyes roll. "Come on, this isn't Twilight."

"No, it's Smoky Falls, and Lex-"

Just then, the haunting howl of a wolf rises from the

forest, loud and clear, raising the hairs on my arms and the back of my neck.

The guys exchange a loaded look. "We're out of time," Jared says to Milo.

He nods and heads for the door, with the other two following. My feet are frozen to the tile floor and I watch them incredulously. So what, we're going to go outside and they're going to 'poof' and turn into furry animals?

Milo holds the door and looks back at me with a fiery glint in his eyes. "Well, are you coming outside or not?"

Chapter Seventeen

LAYLA

~

I can't believe I'm doing this.

I follow the guys outside, where they immediately begin stripping their clothes off.

Now it's not as if I have no desire to gaze at their toned, athletic bodies rippling under the moonlight, but when they start unbuttoning jeans and kicking off shoes, my virginal instincts kick in immediately. My eyes drop to my shoes and I shield my vision with a hand.

"Oh my god, if this is just some trick to get me to run naked with you and end up having an orgy, I will never forgive you!" I hiss, afraid to raise my voice for fear of attracting the wild animals in the woods.

But none of them reply. A pained noise from Landon

has me peeking around my fingers to check on him, and then I can't stop staring.

All three of them have dropped to their hands and knees on the expansive lawn, their bodies contorting painfully, and they face away from me toward the moon. It's a clear night, and although the moon isn't full, it's plenty bright for me to see what's happening.

Disturbing movement under the skin of their backs is the first thing that catches my eye. Stretching shapes, then loud snapping sounds, low painful cries from all three of them, and I just watch in horror.

In perfect sync, their bodies lengthen, widen, their legs shortening and changing shape, as fur sprouts across their skin. Tails erupt from all three of their backsides, and when they tilt their heads back to bay at the moon a moment later, it is from three perfectly canine faces. Their howls join a chorus of similar noises from the forest, and although a low whine emits from the grey wolf that was Landon a moment ago, these wolves do not take off to join the others.

I back up, heart pounding, until my body presses against the rough stone wall of the house. All three of them sit calmly and observe me, waiting.

The wolf-formerly known-as-Milo is especially fluffy with midnight fur, a single grey paw the only break in his pitch-black coloring. The Jared wolf is brown, a rich chocolate color with a lighter mask. Landon's wolf is mostly light grey, with a darker saddle pattern on his back.

I keep staring at them, and they continue waiting.

Swallowing desperately because my mouth is suddenly dry, I mutter, "Well, that's new. You weren't kidding."

The Milo wolf barks a laugh of acknowledgement. Even like this, I can see their intelligence, feel their distinct personalities, like auras that surround them. If my eyes were closed and they shuffled around, I'd know which went where without even peeking to see. I just *feel* them.

And I can feel that they are not wild animals that would attack me. There is no danger here.

This realization sucks the last drop of strength from me. My legs are barely holding me up, so I sink to the porch and take a seat, my breath coming in heavy pants. Slowly, Milo stands, walking toward me with caution as he observes my face for signs of fear.

Truthfully, I'm not afraid of him. That connection, that aura of his presence is like a neon sign blaring that it's the same Milo I was kissing just hours ago. As freaky as it is that they just turned into animals before my eyes—*literally*—it also makes sense in some strange part of my mind that I'm trying desperately to listen to. Like my practical, no-nonsense side tells me it's impossible, but some core part of me knew all along and is glad the rest of me finally caught up.

I put my hand out like I would a skittish dog I want to pet, and he approaches, pressing his furry head into my palm. It's even softer than I imagined, and when I scratch behind his ears he seems to enjoy it, a low hum rumbling in his chest.

"You can come up, too," I tell Jared and Landon, and

Jared leaps forward with his tongue lolling out, eager to claim my other hand for pets. Landon creeps up behind and delicately rests his chin on my leg.

"So, this is new," I observe. A minute ago I was with three hot guys. Now I'm surrounded by three furry wolves.

And even though my logical mind tells me it should feel different, it feels exactly the same.

My breathing evens out, my heart rate dropping to a normal level, and we sit quietly together.

In the distance, the other group of wolves howls and yips, running further into the forest. But I stay on the porch, content now that I understand at least a *part* of this story. I sit, surrounded by their warmth, my fingers busy petting while I'm lost in thought.

I don't know how much time has passed when another howl sounds in the distance, and Landon sits up, his head tilted to one side. Whining softly, he turns to Milo, who huffs in acknowledgement. He leans in to bump his head against my cheek, then all three of run off the porch.

"Wait!" I call, jumping to my feet and planning to race after them.

But they don't go far. Just off the porch, they pause by the piles of their belongings, then whimper in unison.

As if I'm watching a rewind of what I witnessed earlier, the three wolves slowly turn back into the guys I knew. No more tails, fur, or fuzzy ears.

Once again they're fully human, and fully naked, so

I avert my eyes while they get dressed, staring instead at the moon. For some reason, I feel like she's speaking to me, only in a language I don't understand. Just like the guys, the moon seems to have an aura that means something, but I can't quite put my finger on what it is.

"Ahem." Milo's quiet voice startles me and I jump before glancing down to realize they're all dressed and staring at me, once again, waiting.

"So, that was interesting," I prompt. "I assume you have more to tell me?"

"Yeah, there's... definitely more to tell. Can we go back up to your room and talk?"

The quiet night has suddenly become eerie, and a chill that has nothing to do with the weather licks up my spine. "Yeah, I think that's a good idea."

We make our way through the dark house and back up to my suite. I claim a corner of the couch and a furry throw blanket, then settle back. "Alright, out with it."

Landon and Jared both look at Milo for guidance, who sighs. "You know, I don't know how I became the spokesman here, but at some point, you guys are gonna need to speak up."

"You're just so much better at it," Landon grins.

"Exactly," Jared agrees. "Always have been."

"Practice makes perfect," Milo grumbles, but he returns his gaze to me. "Okay, I'll tell you what I can, but I need you to understand I can't tell you everything."

"Why not? Surely the cat's out of the bag now... or, I suppose, I should say dog."

"Wolf, please, we're not dogs."

"Fine, the wolf is out of the bag."

"It's not that simple. The alpha, your uncle, decreed-"

"Wait, Uncle Dom is the *alpha*? That's like, the leader, right? Now it all makes sense. I thought he had way too much going on for a mayor of such a small town."

"Yes, he's the alpha. And he decreed no one could talk to you about the pack until-"

"Well, how are you talking to me about it, then?"

"Lex, if you would please let me get a word in, I'd *love* to explain it to you."

"Sorry," I mime zipping my lips. "Go on."

Milo sighs. "So, the alpha decreed that no one can tell you about the pack to keep someone from accidentally spilling the beans before he wanted you to know. He charged *us* with telling you about our wolves for a specific reason, but even we aren't allowed to give you a lot of details."

"So what's the reason, and what are you supposed to tell me?"

Milo pauses. "There aren't only *three* wolves in this room, Lex."

"What? Who else is here?" I look around, not seeing anyone beside the three of them.

And then I catch on. "*Me*? I'm a wolf too?"

All three of them nod soberly. "Yes," Milo confirms.

The world seems to tilt on its axis. "If that's true, how come I've never changed into a wolf before?"

"There's a manifestation ceremony that takes place, typically the first full moon of your seventeenth year. But you can only shift on this land. Smoky Falls is special; it's magically protected. So, because you weren't here before now, you've never been able to have the manifestation. There's not much more to it."

"So at the next full moon…" I whisper, following along while horror drops in my stomach.

"You'll manifest," Milo finishes. "Exactly."

"When is that?" I'd never been good at keeping up with moon cycles.

"Friday is your ceremony," Landon speaks up, his voice soft.

"You guys already know? Who are the wolves in this town, anyway? Does everyone know? Who were all those wolves in the forest?" The questions fire from my lips like machine-gun bullets, spraying in all directions.

"The entire town is our pack. All of them are wolves, and anyone over seventeen who has manifested can join the alpha in the woods for a run at midnight. Not everyone goes every night, but it's the only time we can shift, and… it's just in our nature. We have to shift every so often, run with the alpha, reconnect with the pack."

"Wow, okay. I guess now I know why I hear wolves every night. So… is that why my mom ran away, because she didn't want to be a wolf? I'm assuming that's how you know I'm one?"

Milo swallows hard, his Adam's apple bobbing painfully. "I can't answer questions about your mom.

I'm sorry Lex. I didn't know her. You'll have to ask your uncle. But our job was to make sure you know what you are, and that you're ready to manifest on Friday."

A sliver of fear strikes my chest. "How much does it hurt? It looked super painful when you guys... changed. Will you be there? Is this something I have to do on my own with like a priest or something? Will I still be me when I'm a wolf?"

Jared reaches for my hand and squeezes it with warm fingers. "We'll be there. The entire town will. It hurts a little, the first time is the worst. But it goes away as soon as the shift is done. And yes, you'll still be you, gorgeous."

"The ceremony isn't as complicated as it sounds," Landon adds. "It's more about everyone witnessing that you are a wolf, part of the pack, then running together for your first run. Sort of like a community event. Every full moon we all run together, and if there's a manifestation that month, we do that too."

A few things click into place. "Wait a second. You guys took your clothes off to change... I have to change into a wolf in front of the *whole town*. Does that mean I have to strip naked in front of the *entire town*?" My voice rises to a squeak and panic blossoms in my chest. Why this is freaking me out more than the idea that I'm going to turn into a giant canine? I have no idea.

"You don't have to," Landon rushes to reassure me. "A lot of people will bring a change of clothes to their manifestation. When you shift, if you don't undress, you kind of just burst out of your clothes. So it doesn't matter if you don't take them off first, they'll just be destroyed. We took ours off so we didn't waste a perfectly good set of clothes, and once you've done it a few times, you just kind of get used to getting naked."

"Yeah, you can just wear some crappy clothes you don't care about and bring a spare set to change," Jared agreed. "That's what I did. I didn't want the entire town, let alone Amber, staring at my junk."

A snort escapes my nose. "Has she been after you that long?"

"Oh yeah," Landon laughs. "Amber's been on his junk since we were thirteen. I bet she's *pissed* you came back."

Milo smacks his arm and gives him a warning look, but it's too late. I already caught on.

"What does that have to do with me? He clearly doesn't want her, regardless of whether I'm here or not." I don't mention the fact that I already hooked up with Milo. A thread of guilt wriggles in my belly... I certainly hope Jared isn't expecting something from me. I like him, of course, but if I start dating Milo I don't want him to be hurt.

"I think Landon just meant that's why she's jealous," Milo supplies quickly. "Since he never hangs out with her, and we've been with you since the first day you arrived."

Suspicion floods my thoughts, and I narrow my eyes at the three of them. "Yeah, why is that, anyway?"

"Why is what?" Jared asks.

"Why have you guys been on me since day one? Is

this all some sort of assignment from Dom or Roxanne?" My brain zips straight to memories of the intense embarrassment from the first day of classes, when Jared let slip that Roxanne gave them my schedule so I wouldn't be alone.

Jared's eyes widen in horror. "No! Not at all. I mean, yes, they want us all to get along, but it's deeper than that. We feel it, and I know you feel the connection to us."

"I do, but I don't understand what that is."

Milo sighs. "Lex, I'm sorry, that's one of the things we can't explain at this moment. But I promise you'll get a lot more answers after the manifestation on Friday."

I glare at him, but he just looks back at me glumly. "Trust me, I'd love to tell you, but I physically can't."

A snort escapes me in a loud huff. "I get being afraid of getting in trouble, but this is a bit much."

"No, it's not that," Jared interjects, his dark eyes sincere. "The alpha has some powers, and one of them is the alpha command. If he decrees something, we physically *can't* disobey him. He forbade the entire pack from speaking to you about the pack, period. He gave us special permission to prepare you for manifestation, and that is all."

Resentment rises in my chest, the heat of my fury filling my body with energy. "You know, this is all kind of bullshit. Why didn't he tell me all of this himself? I've been in this house with him every night since I arrived, he could have picked *any* of those times to lay it all out.

Why doesn't he just give me answers now? What would it harm? I'm going to ask him." Throwing back the blanket, I stand and march toward the suite door, the guys scrambling to their feet in my wake.

Even though it's dark in the hallway, I am familiar enough with this house to know where I'm going. First I throw open the office door, but it's dark inside, so I move on to my uncle's suite of rooms. I've never knocked on this door, but I swallow down the nerves and bang loudly. The guys are a few steps away as if they fear the doors will fly open and he'll shoot flames from his mouth like an angry dragon.

I wait several minutes, but he doesn't appear. Frustrated, I try the knob, but it's locked.

"Argh, where the hell is he?" I growl, my brain firing for an idea of where he might be.

Brushing past the guys, I walk back down the hallway and push my way into the library.

There's no fire, just a few candles, but sure enough my uncle is on the couch reading.

The guys wait in the doorway, but I march in and stand in front of him.

My uncle doesn't look up. "I see you boys completed your mission." His voice is low and neutral, a slight note of amusement the only sign of emotion.

"Yes, alpha," Milo answers in a similarly neutral voice, devoid of amusement.

"Good job. Now you should return to your homes. You'll see Layla in the morning at class."

"Goodbye, Layla."

"Bye, Lex."

"See you tomorrow."

Just like that, without a second's hesitation, they're gone. The sense of betrayal is strong and fuels my anger at my uncle.

I watch them depart into the darkness, then turn back to the man himself, placidly reading on the couch, with an incredulous expression. "Who *are* you?"

He sighs, then looks at me for the first time. "I'm your uncle, your mother's brother, and I'm the alpha of the Smoky Falls pack."

"That's why you think you can just boss people around? Because you're an alpha? What about-"

"Yes," he cuts me off sharply. "I can boss people around *precisely* because I'm the alpha. It's called compulsion, and I, and to a lesser extent my beta, can use it to manage the pack. Sometimes it's the only way to make sure everyone continues working for the harmony and betterment of the pack."

"By taking away their free will?" I snap. "That seems pretty shitty to me."

"I understand why you feel that way. Your mother also disliked the idea of alpha compulsion. But we only use it when necessary, I assure you. I couldn't have the town telling you about us before you were ready to hear it. I wanted to make sure the news came from someone you connected to, someone who felt like a friend. That's why I chose those three to tell you."

"Who's we?"

"Excuse me?"

"You said 'we only use it.' Who is we?"

"I told you, me, and my beta."

"And who is your beta?"

"I should have thought that was obvious. She's here all the time. Roxanne is my beta."

The realization zooms in on me with the force of a Mack truck.

Roxanne is the beta, and she can use compulsion.

My constant need to do what she wanted, to obey, to throw myself into my studies for the year we were in LA, to follow every order for my physical therapy.

To ignore the pangs in my heart telling me to go back to North Hollywood, to obey and stay with her.

That was all her using compulsion on me, controlling me, making me think it was my own free will.

Bile rises in my throat. All this time, I thought she was helping me. I thought she genuinely cared about me and wanted me to be safe and happy.

Turns out she was just controlling me, on my uncle's orders.

"You need to tell me everything. There's clearly a ton that's been left out here, and I want answers. *Now*."

Dom just chuckles. "You presume to command *me*? That's cute. But no. You'll get your answers when I say. *After* you complete the manifestation and you're officially part of the pack, you'll get all the answers you need. I can compel you to stop asking, but I'd rather not. It takes a lot of energy and I'm already expending a good deal, keeping the entire village from telling you everything."

I stare at him with the fire of my fury for a moment, and he gazes neutrally back at me.

"What if I don't want to become a wolf? What if I leave before the full moon, like my mom did?"

My uncle doesn't rise to the challenge. "Well, technically you're an adult so I can't keep you here. But all of this," he gestures around him, indicating the castle and of course the money, clothes, and everything he's provided for me, "stays here. You can't be a member of the pack, receive benefits of the pack, and not be a wolf. But it's certainly your choice to make."

It's an impossible choice: Accept the fact that I'm going to turn into a giant wolf in four days, that it will likely be incredibly painful, and that I'll be compelled forever to do it every so often to remain a member of the pack.

Or walk out the door and go right back to living on the streets.

Part of me wants to shuck up my big girl panties and leave right now. I lived on the street before, I can do it again. My mom left all of this behind and never looked back. And I have a high school diploma (sort of) now; I'm an adult, with a driver's license. I can get a job.

But the bizarre sense of never belonging in California, despite living there my entire life, finally makes sense. From the moment I crossed onto this property, I felt a warm, reassuring sense of belonging—this is my *home*. This connection I have to the pack is real, and deep within my soul. I can't imagine leaving it all behind now, leaving the guys behind, just cutting myself off from them completely. Not to mention I'm actually enjoying college (mean girl drama aside) and love the idea of having access to as many books as I could ever want to read.

My uncle watches me quietly, the self-assured smile on his lips aggravating the shit out of me. He knows he has me trapped. I wondered why I'd suddenly found such good fortune when he swept me off the streets, and now I finally see it. It comes with some pretty serious strings attached, of the canine variety.

I know I'm not leaving, and he knows it, too.

"Fine," I sigh, scraping my fingers through my hair. "But after the manifestation on Friday, I get *all* the answers. Agreed?"

"Absolutely," he grins. "You have my word."

Chapter Eighteen

LAYLA

~

No lie, going to classes the next day is an experience.

Knowing what I know now forces me to see people in a different light. The guys said everyone in town is a member of the pack. That means they *all* obey my uncle, and they all know about the wolf stuff to which I was completely ignorant until last night.

And they all know that, too.

Thinking back on it now, it's humiliating to realize everyone was in on the secret except me. I walk the halls and wonder how many people desperately want to tell me the truth, but are held back by Uncle Dom's alpha command. Whether for benevolent or nefarious reasons, I have to imagine there are plenty of people who would speak up, if they could.

Of course, that will all be over in just a few days. Friday is the full moon, and then all the secrets will be out.

All the extra attention makes sense now, too. Of course people would be curious. The niece of the alpha suddenly shows up and has no clue about this world. When we sit down for lunch and Savannah joins us, I let her know that I'm in on the secret now.

"Oh thank goddess, obviously I wanted to tell you, but I couldn't disobey the alpha command. And your manifestation is this Friday! You must be so nervous. I about made myself sick beforehand, and lordy the pain of the first shift, it was unimaginable!"

My eyes grow wide as she rambles and when she pauses, her gaze locks on something over my shoulder. I whip around to catch Jared making a 'cut' gesture across his brown neck with one hand.

"You said it's not that bad." I glare at him accusingly.

"Pain is relative," Savannah rushes to explain. "It's really not *that* bad. I just was so worked up it seemed to go on forever and I'd never experienced that kind of pain before. I mean, it hurts like a bitch *every* time we shift. It doesn't really get better, you just get used to it." She smiles encouragingly, and I have lost all of my appetite.

"Great." I push my plate away and cross my arms over my stomach, the nerves swirling within keeping me plenty full.

Savannah keeps frantically trying to fix her mistake.

"Oh man, I'm sorry. I've really put my foot in it. It's just —we all grow up knowing about it, so we spend our whole life preparing for it. I can't imagine what it'd be like going in completely unprepared. I mean, you've only been here a week. That's gotta be extra stressful."

I know she's trying to make me feel better, but she's only succeeding in worsening the cramps in my belly.

"I think that's probably enough talking about the manifestation," Milo hints. "It won't do Lex any good to stress about it for the next few days, and despite our fears, we all come through just fine."

Milo's statement is a warm balm to my upset stomach, and my heart slows a bit.

"Oh, yeah, that's totally true!" Savannah agrees. "Thinking about it was *way* worse than the actual manifestation. In the weeks leading up, I was such a nervous wreck I-"

"She doesn't need the details, Savannah," Milo asserts. "And we should probably head to our next class."

Finally taking the hint, Savannah nods. "Yeah, okay. I'll see you guys later!" She hops up and walks away, and I gather my things.

"Don't bother, we've got another twenty minutes before class," Milo mutters without looking away from his phone. "I just gave her an excuse to make a quick exit."

"Very clever of you," I reply with a smirk. "I like her, but sometimes I feel like she's a bit much to handle. Even though she means well, I find her exhausting."

"Funny, I always find her presence calming," Landon shrugs. "I think because when she's around, she talks so much it takes the pressure off of me to say anything."

"Ha! That's true," Jared agrees. "She does tend to fill all the silences. But I personally have never had a problem. Hey Lex, why do seagulls fly over the ocean?"

My lips curl into a tiny smile. "I dunno, Jared, why do seagulls fly over the ocean?"

"Because if they only flew over the harbor, they'd be called bagels! Get it, bay-gulls?"

I snort a laugh, but Milo groans. "I think that was your worst one yet, man."

"No, man," Landon disagrees. "His worst one is definitely still the pirate one."

"Which is the pirate one?" Now I'm curious.

Jared's dark eyes turn to me. "What's a pirate's favorite letter?"

I shrug. "I dunno, R? Like Argghh?" I affect a poor pirate accent, and Jared's grin widens.

Gleefully, he answers, "No, it's the C!"

Now I actually chuckle. "That was clever. That can't be the worst one."

"Jesus, don't encourage him," Landon gripes. "Once he gets on a roll, he won't stop."

"Hey, there are worse things than enjoying a cheesy joke," Jared protests. "I dunno why you guys hate on them so much. It's just harmless fun."

"Jared, I love you, but those jokes are neither 'fun'

nor 'harmless.' You should find a new hobby." Milo shakes his head as if he's disappointed.

"What, like drinking energy drinks and playing Minecraft? Pass. I'll stick to football and corny jokes."

Landon's expression goes slack, as if he's offended. "Hey don't knock Minecraft, it's fun and millions of people play it. And most people like energy drinks in some form."

"Not me, I'll stick to coffee," Milo interjects.

"Isn't that kind of like an energy drink, though?"

Milo looks affronted. "Certainly not. It's coffee, brewed from beans. Therefore, *natural*. Your drinks are chemical-laden and produced in a lab with tons of sugar and shit like yellow-47."

"You're one to talk about sugar, mister flat white with 3 packets of sugar," Jared elbows him in the ribs.

"Yeah, well, at least it's all natural sugar and real milk." Milo sniffs. "You can't shame me about my coffee, so give it up."

"Hey, how about we all just live and let live?" I ask. "You guys seem rather judgy about each other."

The guys glance at each other in silence for a moment. "You know we're just messing around, right?" Jared asks carefully. "We're about as close as three guys can possibly be. I mean that in the best way," he adds quickly, as if I might infer something.

"Yeah, we give each other crap, but it's all in good fun," Landon adds. "We've grown up together, shared everything we've had ever practically since we were born."

Landon's eyes are serious, seemingly laden with meaning as he says that last part.

My mind immediately whips back to kissing Milo last night, then Landon's clever, soulful eyes taking in my fingers intertwined with Milo's on the couch. Surely he's not implying they'd share... *that?*

Milo takes the opportunity to change the subject. "Alright, pack it up. We really need to get to class now."

Heat rushes through me, but I decide to take the 'now or never' approach to testing this new theory. The three boys wait for me to pass through the door into the hallway, and when Milo emerges I reach for his hand. That sexy, one-sided smile curls his lips as he accepts, threading his fingers through mine.

Then when Landon falls into step on my other side, I slip my hand into his as well. It's larger than Milo's, with the long fingers of someone who should be seriously good at basketball. Landon glances down at me in surprise, his cheeks coloring lightly pink and a pleased smile taking up residence on his lips.

Not wanting Jared to feel left out, I glance over my shoulder and blow him a kiss, earning a wide grin and a wink in reply.

Sharing, indeed.

Layla

For the rest of the week, I avoid telling anyone else that I know about the manifestation, for fear they would make it sound even worse than it already did. Somehow I survive to Friday, ride home with Maxwell to Harridan House, and sit through a surprisingly full dinner. Now that the household staff knows I'm aware of the wolves, they've also been a lot more relaxed around me. My uncle graces me with his presence for dinner even though it's not Sunday, and tonight we eat with all the staff, as well as several of their families and some landscapers in the cavernous, ornate formal dining room.

Roxanne is here, and all the guys come with their parents. There's a decidedly festive atmosphere to the dinner, and it's served buffet style so everyone can help themselves and enjoy the food with no need for serving. Once again I get the feeling that there's more going on than I'm aware—surely they don't have this kind of celebration for every manifestation?—but it might just be because of my unique circumstances. I am the alpha's niece and family seems to be a big deal here. Not to mention my status as a missing person for so long.

The guys' parents all beam at me whenever we make eye contact, and the boys themselves are always nearby. I take comfort in their presence, as I have all week at SFC. I've experimented with more hand-holding, often two of them at once, and continue to get the electric thrill with every touch of their skin on mine. If the other students think our little group is odd, they certainly don't react. Perhaps there is truth to the guys' insistence that they've shared everything since they were born. I wonder if they've ever shared a girlfriend before…

Not that I consider myself their girlfriend, of course. Just wondering how they seem to be so at ease with it. The excitement of flirting with three hot guys at once is sort of damped by the complete lack of apparent jealousy—which also makes me question if I'm just reading too much into it. Milo and I kissed that one time, but other than some hand-holding, we haven't had any more contact, and I certainly haven't kissed either of the other two yet. Until I know more about how *much* they actually share, I'm not going to press my luck.

But they all seem happy and excited for me tonight, just like all the attendees at this surprise soiree. So I brush off the trepidation and allow the party to do its work, relaxing me from fears of the impending ceremony with a celebratory atmosphere.

Dinner goes later than usual, since everyone is hanging out until the ceremony. All I've been told is that it takes place at the stroke of midnight when the moon is full, then everyone shifts and goes for a run as a pack. The guys couldn't tell me much more, other than running together is essential to keep pack harmony.

The party eventually breaks up, with some disappearing in twos and threes to clean up the kitchen, or take care of some other evening errand before the main excitement.

The guys and I head up to my suite to watch tv while my uncle chats with their parents. I try to ignore it, but I can't stop myself from glancing at the clock face on my phone repeatedly. Even though it's digital and there isn't a single mechanical clock in my rooms, the ticking seems to get louder with every passing minute.

Milo claims my fingers, forcing me to drop my phone in my lap as he presses a kiss to the back of my hand and sends tiny shoots of electricity racing across my skin. When I scoop the phone with my right hand, Jared copies the move, pulling my hand into his lap and tracing absent-minded patterns into my palm. Between these two and Landon, whose head takes up most of my leg space, I'm penned in on all sides by their comforting presence. I sigh loudly, then try extra hard to focus on the show and ignore the urge to check the time.

Finally, Roxanne knocks on my door and tells us it's time to go. She smiles warmly at me, but I just heft my bag of spare clothes and brush past her. The hurt is still fresh, and I'm pissed that she used compulsion on me before I even knew what it was.

Her hopeful expression falls, and she holds the door wide for the guys to follow me. We make our way down the stairs and onto the back lawn, following the stream of bodies through the garden paths.

Obviously, they know where they're going, even though I'm the person who lives here and has no clue about any of this. The fear I've been suppressing for the last several days resurfaces with a vengeance, elevating my heart rate and setting my stomach sloshing with acid.

Always sensitive to my feelings, Milo snags my left hand, and Jared takes my bag, passing it to Landon, before claiming my right hand. Landon walks directly behind me, and their closeness bolsters my shaky nerves. I focus on the warm electric currents from their closeness and try to tune out the uncomfortable clenching of my stomach.

I shouldn't be surprised when we veer off the path into the forest in the exact spot where I'd seen the wolf print. This is clearly an entrance of sorts, and once we leave the wood-chip trail, the path through the trees is clear. It's wide enough for the guys to remain by my sides, and we join a continuous flow of people heading in the same direction.

I don't want to think about exactly how many people are going to be there to witness my transformation. A fervent prayer rolls in my mind, pleading that I'm sufficiently transformed and no longer very human-looking when I eventually burst through my clothes. A smaller, but not less fervent hope is there also, that it might not hurt *quite* as much as everyone says.

The path narrows, and Jared steps back to join Landon, leaving only Milo by my side. Eventually we approach the main body of the group, the low rumbling of their whispered conversations a steady hum among the trees. We join the throng that are passing through the bottleneck and spreading in a circle around the exterior of a clearing. More people, I can see, are joining from all sides, having passed through the woods to meet us here. I wonder vaguely if they have gps points programmed into their phones, or they just use some kind of wolfy sense to find the right spot.

It's a simple forest clearing, nothing man made or noteworthy here. In the absolute middle stand my uncle and Roxanne, and everyone else affords them a good deal of space. I'm toward the back of the exterior circle, the guys once again reclaiming my hands, and Landon pressed gently at my back. I glance around and can see people deep in the trees, standing in the darkness, just waiting.

Gulping down my nerves, I turn my attention back to my uncle, who stands smiling benevolently in the circle. I try to keep my mind from calculating exactly how many people are out there.

It's bright in the clearing, and I realize the full moon is almost directly overhead. Everyone the light touches is leached of color, looking like so many shades of black, white, and grey. My uncle's shirt is bone white, Roxanne's skin nearly the same ebony as her hair in the dramatic contrast. Randomly observing helps ease my nerves, so I focus on visuals and shut my mind to intruding thoughts of pain.

As if they receive a signal that I don't, everyone ceases talking at once.

Uncle Dom's smile widens, and I suck in a sharp breath. *This is it.* My heart races even faster than before, and I try to swallow away my suddenly dry throat.

"Greetings, Smoky Falls pack! Another month, and

another manifestation ceremony for us. Manifestation is always a cause to celebrate! There's nothing more important than our youth becoming adults by our traditional standards. However, this one is special for us, as it involves my niece, Layla Harridan. Come forward, Layla!" Picking me out of the crowd, my uncle gestures in my direction and the group parts before me like the Red Sea for Moses.

The guys both squeeze my hands, and Landon gives me the bag of clothes with an encouraging palm on my shoulder.

Fighting the nerves, I adopt my street-tough, 'nothing bothers me' attitude and march to the center of the circle. The silence is absolutely deafening as many of the townspeople get their first look at me. I feel their eyes raking over my body from head to toe, and if they think I am the spitting image of my mother, they don't say a peep. Deathly silence surrounds me in the clearing, the only noise the light breeze through the trees and the crunch of my steps on the forest floor.

My uncle embraces me with a hug that feels forced, then turns me around and rests a hand on my shoulder. My heart rate continues to climb; deep in my bones, I know this is right. I belong here, doing this *right now*.

But something else inside me is issuing a blaring warning to run.

"As you know, Layla just returned to us this month. So even though it is her manifestation, she's already eighteen." That sets them talking. I can see the shocked expressions as they whisper back and forth. "It's not common, but it has happened before that someone doesn't manifest exactly on time. It doesn't make a difference, it's always the same.

"Now, I understand we have two others for whom tonight is their manifestation? Please come forward."

Two teenagers, both as nervous-looking as I feel, step into the circle clutching bags of their own. One's a shapely girl with blonde hair, one a skinny boy with black pants and eye makeup. "Wonderful, come closer, please. The ceremony is the same for all three of you."

The others approach with trepidation—I can practically see them shaking, their shoulders hunched as they cower. Strange. I'm nervous about the ceremony, but they look absolutely terrified. I thought Savannah said they grow up knowing this will happen, so it's not that big of a deal?

Patting my shoulder once, my uncle releases me and presses me gently toward the center of the circle. "You may drop your belongings in the middle, then please face out, back to back, so the pack may bear witness to your first shift."

We pile our bags between us, then do as instructed, forming a triangle as we each face a different direction. I make a point of facing the direction I'd come, so I can see Milo, Jared, and Landon's faces in the crowd. They've pushed to the front, and their encouraging smiles give me strength. *I watched them do this; I trust them, and they told me I can do it, too.*

I'll be just fine. I glance up at the full, glorious moon, and soak in her comforting aura.

Uncle Dom and Roxanne step away, and in a smug tone, he says, "It's time."

At that moment, a thousand cell phone alarms ring out through the forest.

Chimes, beeps, digital songs as well as fully recorded music all blend in an absolute cacophony that instantly gives me a splitting headache.

Why the fuck do they all have their alarms going off at once? Why don't they shut them off, now that they've sounded? The noise muddles my head, and I squeeze my eyes shut to keep them from bugging out of their sockets.

Then the first sharp pain lances across my back, forcing me down to all fours in agony, and I realize with shock that the ceremony has already begun.

Chapter Nineteen

LAYLA

❧

All the sounds in my ears have become one massive, howling scream of noise. I can't distinguish anything. I'm too busy being torn apart from the inside.

Now, all the individual snaps, pops, and breaks as my bones shift and reform, my body rapidly expanding and changing—all of those I hear, I *feel*, in perfect, agonizing clarity.

Every one of my fingers, the knuckles popping, doubling under and shrinking.

Every one of my ribs wrenching from my spine and growing, widening, then pushing back into place.

Especially the bones in my legs, shortening and breaking and bending backwards to accommodate an all-fours canine shape instead of an upright human shape.

I even feel my pelvis snap, twisting and tilting to change form.

I want to scream. I want to release a litany of curses and perhaps unload some of this agony by pouring it from my mouth.

But I can't make a sound. All I can do is hold on, try to keep my body in one place as it continues breaking and expanding.

Suddenly the pain subsides, and I can lift my head. But when I can finally unleash the screams I've been holding in, they don't come out as human noises of suffering. A high, mournful howl pours from my lips, and when I open my eyes, I'm looking down a long white muzzle to the full moon directly overhead.

Behind me, two more voices form a chorus, and I howl again to commiserate in our shared agony.

But Jared was right; the pain is gone now. My new body feels slightly foreign, but I'm able to stand and trot in a tight circle. I whip around, catching sight of something that stays tantalizingly on the edge of my vision as I circle. It takes me several attempts before I realize I am literally chasing my tail.

I promise right now to never call a dog dumb again.

"The manifestation ceremony was successful! You have all witnessed these three become members of our pack. Now, let's all change and enjoy our pack run." My uncle's voice cuts through my distraction and I cast my eyes in his direction. All around me, people are stripping off their clothes, and I can see it in exquisite detail.

Too much detail. My wolf eyes are sharp, lightening the shadows and revealing each individual of the crowd spread out through the trees as clear as day. I can feel them, every person in the pack, and I allow my senses to steer me toward the guys.

Landon, Jared, and Milo are already mid-shift, and it doesn't take them long to complete it. Once furry, they bound over to me and we set about nuzzling and bumping into each other in a familial way. A thrum of contentment rumbles in my throat, and we continue the furry affection until a sharp, commanding bark draws our attention immediately.

All around us, every wolf has turned their furry heads and is pointed directly at a large white wolf with a single black ear.

I know without thinking that is my uncle, and I know he's compelling me to stand with him. The push is gentle but impossible to ignore. I trot up to his side, and he gives me a nudge toward the path that leads further into the forest.

Once again the crowd parts, and I start forward hesitantly, my uncle by my side. We begin with a slow trot, and then he speeds up a little, and I accept the challenge, growing accustomed to my new body. I can feel the pack behind us, following at a distance, but my eyes are only forward.

Faster and faster my uncle presses me to run, and

we follow a natural curve in the path as we race, our nails digging into the soft soil.

Now that I'm settling into this body, I notice more and more of my surroundings. I can smell so many things, from the subtle rot scent of decaying wood to sweet berries ripening on the bush. Pulling in deep breaths through my nose, I try to categorize more of the scents. It's instinct. Once I separate them from the others, I know what they are. Earthy mushrooms, sharp pine, salamanders and moss and a thousand little creatures in the forest.

We continue racing. My tongue lolls from the side of my mouth now, and I push forward exuberantly, the breeze on my face like no kind of freedom I've ever experienced.

This is home.

This is right.

This is *good*.

I'm so glad I stayed, if only to experience this!

I can feel my friends behind me, not too far behind. I can also sense Roxanne between us and them. The rest of the pack stretches far behind us, so far they fade into the mist of my senses.

Abruptly, we turn a corner and I pull up short; we're back at the clearing. I pick up the scent of a thousand wolves, and see the clothes everywhere, our bags piled in the center.

My every instinct tells me to stop, and I follow without thinking. I dig my claws into the earth and allow them to drag and slow my momentum. Soon, Roxanne comes charging through the path I just exited, all black and silver in the moonlight. Not far behind her are the guys, and they gather around me once more. As the rest of the pack begins to arrive, I search for my uncle and realize I've lost sight of him. My eyes dart among the throngs of wolves pouring into the clearing, but I don't spot another remotely of his coloring. Reaching out with my senses, I realize I can't feel him, either.

Suddenly, all the warm, joyful emotions I had earlier dissipate. A dark, sinister feeling replaces them, and I know I'm not the only one to sense it. My friends form a protective half-circle behind me, their fur standing on end. A prickly feeling spreads across my skin and a low growl emits from my throat.

My eyes travel around the clearing, and to my shock, I realize the group is divided. Roxanne and a majority of the wolves have gathered around me in a cluster, flanking the protective wall of fur at my back.

But before me is a not insignificant group of wolves that look positively feral.

What is this? Where is Uncle Dom? I reach out with my senses once more, but I don't feel him.

Meanwhile, three of the wolves approach, and a sudden wave of realization crashes over me, bringing a strong desire to faint.

My *dreams*.

This is *just* like my dreams, with my uncle disappearing and three wolves coming to attack me. Clearly there's something going on here, some wolf thing that I don't understand, but I have to decide quickly.

A powerful, violent urge to attack rises in my chest, and my head lowers, a deep growl ripping from my throat as I glare at the incomers.

They should hear my warning and take heed.

But they don't.

They continue approaching. My wolf instincts are affronted. How *dare* they presume to encroach when I've already warned them?

My lips pull back, revealing my sharp fangs as a snarl emits from my mouth. Tongue lashing my teeth, I step forward to meet their challenge and give them one final warning.

Stand down or you will regret it, I try to convey without words.

However, I cannot make an impression, and with their own snarls, the three of them pounce on me as one.

The pain of their teeth in my flesh is nothing compared to what I went through in the change. I'm simply overwhelmed by so many teeth, so many claws, so many bodies all coming at me at once.

Overcome, I sink to the ground and emit a high-pitched whine, a plea for help.

A sharp, keening howl rips from the throat of a wolf nearby, and my attackers stop immediately. When they roll away, their cutting teeth are replaced with gentle licks on my nose, head, ears, and I recognize the comforting auras of my guys.

Glancing up, I see wolf Roxanne, standing imperiously above me and glaring at the smaller group of wolves. Instinct kicks in, and I feel the push of her compulsion encouraging me to run home. I stand on shaking legs, and start trotting back the way we came, through the gardens and toward the house. There's no question of getting lost now. I can sense the right path as clearly as if it were a yellow brick road in Dorothy's black-and-white Kansas. The guys trot along with me, and we don't stop running until we reach the doors of Harridan House.

Chapter Twenty

LANDON

~

We follow Layla right up to the house, and since we've all left our belongings in the forest, there's nothing for us to do but shift and avoid staring at each other's bodies until we can find some clothes.

In other words, awkward as fuck.

I know Layla doesn't want to be seen naked. I know she's self-conscious about it. But I am a red-blooded eighteen-year-old guy, and my mate is inches away, stark naked in the cold moonlight.

And she's beautiful.

Her skin glimmers in the pale light, dark hair tumbling over her shoulders to conveniently conceal her breasts.

It takes a massive force of will to prevent my eyes

from dropping lower.

"Are you okay?" I focus on her eyes. They're huge and luminous, practically glowing.

Layla is clearly doing her best to avoid dropping her gaze below my belly button as well. Her cheeks are fiery red, but she sets her chin in determination to keep her eyes on mine. "Something tells me that the last bit was not supposed to happen. What the hell was that?"

She didn't answer my question, but she may as well have. The anxiety rolls off her in waves, and the instinct to comfort her is strong. I wish I had pockets to shove my hands into because all they want to do is wrap around her and I have to assume the nakedness would make that hella awkward.

"Why don't we go inside? You can get dressed and we'll... figure out some way to cover ourselves. Then we can talk about everything."

"You know, everyone keeps promising they're going to tell me everything, and then shit like this happens and I get *no answers*." Her tone is sharp, commanding, and apparently forgetting her nakedness, she props her hands on her hips. "I want answers, *now*." Her glare makes me feel about two feet tall, and I physically shrink into myself under the weight of it.

"Layla," Jared speaks up gently. "There's no more alpha compulsion on us to keep us from speaking. That means there's nothing preventing us from telling you everything now." His voice grows shaky, and I watch his jaw clench. Obviously, I'm not the only one struggling not to ogle our naked mate. "But standing here in the cold, naked, is probably not the best way to do it. The staff will be back soon, too," he hints.

"Fine," she turns and pushes open the antique door, leaving it ajar for us to follow. "I'm taking the elevator. You all can take the stairs. Feel free to grab some towels or whatever—just no naked junk on my furniture."

The house is still brightly lit, probably with the expectation of continued celebration after the run. Layla stomps off toward the elevator nook under the stairs, and the three of us just stare at her naked backside as it retreats. Her wild hair falls to her mid-back, just above the spot where her waist narrows and her hips flare out again.

She may be tiny, but she's got wicked curves.

"Erm," Jared clears his throat as she walks around the corner out of sight and we regain some semblance of brains. "There's a linen closet just over here that should have some bath towels."

We follow him through the kitchen into a storage room of sorts, and he pulls three large, fluffy towels from a closet that we tie around our waists before heading back to the stairs.

I say a silent prayer of gratitude that I didn't have to ascend the stairs without the towels. I'm close with my brothers, but there's no need to see them from *that* angle.

When we reach Layla's suite, the door is open but her bedroom beyond is closed. We all take our seats and wait for her to emerge, not sure what to say in her absence.

Jared takes the first stab at it. "That was… different."

Milo snorts. "Yeah, I'll say."

"I don't understand. What just happened?" I look between the two of them, wondering if they caught something I didn't.

"It's obvious, isn't it?" Milo's voice is tight, barely restrained, fury rolling from him in waves. "As soon as Lex manifested, she released Dom from the curse, and the asshole took off."

"But that's not how it's supposed to work, right?" Jared's dark face scrunches in confusion. "I thought that only happened spontaneously after the previous alpha *died*. Isn't she supposed to become alpha on the lunar eclipse? Why would it suddenly happen as soon as she manifests?"

"Best I can guess is that because Dom was so weak as an alpha that as soon as Layla was back on pack soil, the magic took over." Milo scrubs a hand over his face. "But you're right, this is totally fucked. Because she's not ready, she doesn't have the alpha voice. You saw it. If it weren't for Roxanne, they would've torn her apart."

"Well, that just means we have three months to get her ready to take over as alpha," Jared says, brimming with positivity. "At least we still have Roxanne. She can't hold the entire pack at bay, but as beta, she has some ability to influence until Layla is ready."

"Yeah, the only problem is that with Dom gone, the curse has fallen to Layla," I groan, slouching in my seat. "And since he took off, it's gonna be on us to explain it to her, like everything else. We're not exactly Harridan descendants, we know piss-all about the fucking thing."

Layla's voice is sharp and clear, freezing me to my seat instantly. "What did you say about a curse?"

∼

Layla

∼

"What did you say about a curse?" I demand again, glaring at the three guilty faces in my living room. "Because this is the first fucking time *I'm* hearing anything about it."

They were waiting for me, harmlessly chatting, and I was sitting on my bed, trying to dispel the icy shivers that hadn't left my body since the attack in the woods.

But I can't resist eavesdropping, especially since they are discussing the night's events and I'm trying to digest the same thing.

"You'd better come sit, Layla. We don't know everything, but we'll tell you everything we can. I promise." Milo's gaze is firm and sincere, and no trace of duplicity in his baby blues. I refuse to let my gaze drop to his bare chest and ogle him right now; I'm too shaken.

Sighing, I cross from my doorway to the big cozy chair and drag the furry blanket over me, pulling my knees to my chest. "I'm listening." It's the most I can give him in this moment. I don't want to touch any of them right now, to let them comfort me with that electric tingle when the floodgates of knowledge have finally been released and I need answers.

Milo settles into his seat, wearing his bath towel skirt just as casually as his typical dress shirts and khakis. "According to our pack history, people who shift into animals have been around since the dawn of man. It helped them survive the elements, find resources, coexist with other animals. Eventually, the ability to shift was lost by most humans, and small pockets of shifters banded together in secrecy, carving out special places, protected by magic.

"As people migrated to the new world, many of them were shifter clans. Our ancestors wanted a fresh start in a more wild place. They brought witches who could tap into the natural magic of specific locations, using that innate power to create sheltered homes for shifters.

"We used to manifest anywhere, but our power is now tied to this land, you understand? That first alpha in Smoky Falls gave something to the earth, and in return, the earth protects us here. We have a magical boundary that keeps non-shifters out. Sure, they can visit, but they never end up with a desire to move here. And as shifters, we don't move anywhere else, lest we lose our ability to shift and our magical bond with the pack.

"So, however many centuries ago in the old world, our pack formed, and we used to have regular dominance fights for leadership. The alpha continuously had to prove themself by deflecting attacks from would-be alphas, and it took much of their time and energy.

"When we moved here, the alpha at the time was part of the witch's spell. From then on, the strength of the pack was tied to that *one* bloodline. That family would always be alpha, otherwise the magic would be broken and this area would no longer be protected. The pack would have to break up, and some might go join other packs or give up being shifters forever.

"I'm sure you're following this by now, but that alpha bloodline is the Harridan bloodline. Your family has been alphas for centuries, and are the only thing keeping this pack together."

Milo clears his throat, obviously uncomfortable, and in a fit of guilt, I run to my mini fridge to grab some drinks for all of us. I'm still angry at all of them, but I'm thirsty, too.

"So I think I'm following that point, but then why did those wolves attack me? Who was that, anyway? And where is my uncle? And I'm *still* waiting for an explanation of this curse."

"I think I ought to take over, if that's alright with you." Roxanne's voice intrudes on our group, and I look up in surprise. She's in the doorway, holding a neat pile of the guys' belongings and my bag from the clearing.

The boys take their things and disappear into my room to change, and Roxanne sits in the chair opposite me. "I'm sorry I couldn't tell you everything before, but I trust by now the boys have told you about the alpha compulsion. I was very limited in what I could share, on your uncle's orders."

Sighing, I nod. "But you can tell me now, right?"

"Yes. So, to answer your question, I need to tell you a little more about your family. It's not just the Harridan bloodline—it's the Harridan *women*. As part of the spell that was worked, the magic that sustains and protects Smoky Falls is passed down through the Harridan females. It renews with each new alpha, who takes her mates and forges fresh connections with the pack, and so the cycle continues."

"Wait, did you say 'mates' as in *plural*?" Something tells me I shouldn't be as surprised as I am.

"Yes, the Harridan alpha always takes three mates. They are designated from birth, and the three mates ensure that the major families of the pack continue to keep equal importance in the pack. There were more, originally, and they constantly fought for the position as alpha. This way the Harridan alpha takes three mates, one from each line, and they become four alphas who share the responsibility of protecting the pack."

"So someone decided who my mates would be at my birth? How is that even possible?"

"In your case, it's a little complicated. It's a magical process, and at the birth of each child, a seer can foretell who each child will mate. You were not born here. There was no seer to designate *your* mates. However, at the birth of three boys, the seer foresaw they would each mate the next Harridan alpha. And here you are."

Icy dread pours over my body like cold water. "And who are those three boys?"

Roxanne tips her head forward, staring into my eyes with meaning. "I think you already know."

And in my heart of hearts, I *do* know. They were too friendly, too nice, too caring. Of course they were only doing it because they *had* to.

"Well, that's great. So literally *no one* is my friend unless they're forced to be." The warm feelings I hold for each of the boys, especially Milo, sours in my stomach. They don't actually want me. They just don't have a choice.

"It's not like that, Layla. I promise. They genuinely care about you. Just because it was foretold by a seer doesn't make those feelings any less real. It's just a magical bond that helps bring us together."

"I... yeah, I don't have space in my head to unpack that right now. Let's get back to my uncle and why those others attacked. And the curse!" I tack on the end.

"Of course. So your uncle was never meant to be alpha—your mother was. However, when she took off before manifesting, she left the pack without an alpha heir. The responsibility passed to your uncle."

"So why didn't he have three mates?"

"Not all shifters that are born in the pack have fated mates. Most do, but some are born without. We encourage them to find a mate among other shifters with no fated mate, or they can choose to join the human world and relinquish their wolf. Because we have so few born in our pack with no fated mate, it's usually their first priority to find a mate among another pack.

"But since your uncle became alpha, he couldn't take a mate from another pack. That would make another bloodline alpha of *our* pack, you understand? It would tear the pack apart from the inside out. Things have been hard enough for him. It's a lot to explain, but your uncle barely possessed enough dominance to hold the position of alpha. He was never meant to lead, and the pack has been in turmoil since the day your mother left. It's truly a miracle you were brought back to us... honestly, I didn't know how much longer he could hold out." Roxanne's eyes drop to her lap. "It seems he left, as soon as you manifested and claimed the position of alpha. It doesn't normally happen that way, no one expected it. But he's been stuck for so long, I think he was just desperate to be free. We have people out looking for him, just to be sure, but I think he may be gone, for good."

For some reason she seems especially saddened by this, way more than an employee should miss their employer. I can't say I'm surprised; I wanted to trust my uncle, but it seems as if people never stay in my life long enough for me to really depend on them, so it's no great loss to me that he's gone. *Except this whole alpha thing...*

Roxanne continues her story. "So he did the best he could, trying to find your mother and bring her back here, before your grandparents died. But he was unsuccessful, and the position as alpha, and the curse, fell to him."

So many tiny pieces click into place.

The portraits in the hall, always one woman and three men.

The three boys in the photos with my mom, one she ran away with and two she abandoned.

"So my mom left behind two of her fated mates? And that's why their kids hate me."

"Yes, the rejection of the bond is painful. It's understandable that it made them bitter, and because your uncle was not as strong, and didn't have mates to help him, he could not keep the pack together as tightly as it should have been. He's struggled under the weight of it. I've done my best to help, but I'm no alpha."

"So that's why he ran away. Now that I'm here, he's finally free to live his life, find a mate. I get it. He said it was too much for him. But I don't *feel* any different? I don't feel like I can command legions or tell anyone what to do? How can I, a girl who just learned about this whole world, be the alpha? What does that even mean?"

"You haven't had your alpha ceremony yet. When the curse on your uncle passed to you, I hesitated to stop the attack. I'm sorry, but I hoped that since you'd replaced him as alpha, you'd just instantly acquire the voice as well. I can see now this situation is far more complicated than we thought."

That word keeps coming back up and it's thick with implication. I give her my steeliest gaze. "That's right, that's something else no one has explained yet. Tell me about this curse."

Chapter Twenty-One

LAYLA

"The curse is… complicated to explain," Roxanne starts hesitantly.

"After everything that's been thrown at me in the last week, I kinda feel like I can keep up."

She sighs. "Okay. So, you know how I said there were four key families in the pack, and the alpha mates a descendant from each to keep each tied in?"

I nod wordlessly, and she continues.

"Well, originally there were eight."

I wait, but she doesn't seem inclined to continue, as if I'm just supposed to understand what that implies.

"Yeah, you're gonna have to give me more than that."

"Before moving to Smoky Falls, we had dominance

battles for the role of alpha. Reasonably, it could switch every full moon—that's when the wolves could challenge for position. It was volatile. There were so many families of equal strength that the alpha hat just got passed around and it was far more wild, far less civilized, than the leadership we have now.

"When we came here, there were no pre-made sanctuaries to work with. The witches figured out how to use our own magic to strengthen the earth magic for protection, and the alpha at the time volunteered herself. What no one realized was that magic tied the earth magic to that blood, not just to the wolves. So the enchantment is only viable so long as someone of that blood is here. The pack voted and agreed that the only solution was for the Harridan family to remain alpha. Each new alpha would take mates from the other families, as many as she could manage, to be 'co-alphas' thus creating harmony and stability in the pack.

"This is when the seers became important. They'd always been used to determine fated mates, which used to be more infrequent but has grown almost inevitable at this point. Prior to that time, if the seer foresaw more than one mate, that person could choose which one to mate and the others sought other mates. Now, she took as many as the seer foretold. The seers began foretelling mates for the alpha children, but it was never over three. More often than not, those three were descendants of the same three families—it was rare that one came from the other four.

"Needless to say, they were not happy about it. The

unrest grew among the pack, and because we had not woven their bloodline in with the alphas as strongly, they eventually could defect and form their own pack. It was a painful split—most people were related to all others however tenuously, so as the pack broke apart it was really people from all eight bloodlines that left, however lightly they were connected.

"But the worst part was that they were vindictive in their departure. Still convinced that we forced them out instead of leaving of their own accord, the Montrose Pack had their witch cast a curse on the Smoky Falls Pack. The alpha, so tied to her lands, could never leave for more than twenty-four hours. And furthermore, she could only shift between the hours of midnight and one am.

"So that's where you find us today. Unfortunately, your surprise manifestation freed Dom from the curse and immediately placed it on you. I don't know if it's because your mother is already gone, or just that Dom was so poorly adept at being alpha that the magic believes you're a better choice. Either way, it's not what we predicted would happen. I'm so sorry, Layla. We had no way of knowing."

My mind spins with all this information. "So you're telling me that not only am I suddenly in charge of this town, and all the people in it, but I'm stuck here? *Forever*?"

"Do you remember how your uncle couldn't come visit you in LA? This is why—he had to be back on the soil in Smoky Falls within twenty-four hours or the magic protecting our land would end, and our pack magic would dissipate. We had to charter a private plane to get him back on time."

"Well boo-hoo for him, I feel so bad about that," I snarl. "But I've just had the responsibility for an entire town, *and* a curse, dropped on me with zero warning. What happens if the magic ends? Why is that so bad?"

"Wolves can only shift on magically protected land. When they go so long without shifting, they lose the ability to shift. Also, the alpha can only maintain a pack on protected land. So there would be no more Smoky Falls Pack."

"Seems like a pretty simple solution to me. Give up the magic, give up this fated mates nonsense, and everyone gets to live the life they want, finally, after all these years."

Roxanne scrubs a hand over her face. "You don't understand. This is our culture, our legacy. We don't have the ability to just walk away from it. In your heart of hearts, you know that. Didn't you feel something, something different, when you came to Smoky Falls? Something you didn't realize was missing until you got here and felt complete?"

I'm too angry with her. I don't want to give her the satisfaction of confirmation. So I just stare blankly at her instead.

Roxanne regards me calmly. "You can't fool me. I know you did. That was your connection to your wolf, your soul, of sorts. If we lose the pack, everyone loses their wolf. Their soul. An essential piece of their makeup will be gone."

"I thought you said that some people who are born without fated mates go live in the human world just fine? Why would this be any different?"

"For one, you're talking about ripping out the part that connects them to their fated. Second, those people who leave do so before they manifest. They might feel a slight emptiness from time to time, but they never bonded with their wolf. For someone who has, it would be like losing an arm or a leg. It doesn't happen very often, but when we banish a wolf from the pack, they typically don't live more than a year."

"What happens to them?" The question is little more than a whisper; I'm afraid to find out.

"They kill themselves, Layla. Without their wolves, they can't find the will to go on. So if a Harridan is not here protecting the pack, you'd essentially be dooming everyone in this town to mental and spiritual torture, and eventually death."

I sit with that information for a minute; the anger roiling in my stomach. So the choice is either I uphold this mantle I had no idea existed before tonight, or I doom everyone to die by their own hands.

That is no choice at all.

Why is the world so fucking unfair? Haven't I struggled enough? Moving constantly with my parents, struggling to make ends meet, year after year, until they were taken from me? And then escaping the horrors of foster care to live on the street, surviving on my instincts with a pack of feral kids, until I'm almost murdered. Then, what seems like a stroke of luck, finding a long-lost, wealthy relative to take me in, only to discover the truth is he planned to dump all of his responsibilities on me the second he was able and stick me with a curse that would prevent me from ever leaving this place for more than a day?

Ironically, my mind drifts to my thoughts of just a few days ago, imagining visiting the Eiffel Tower or the pyramids in Egypt, but still wanting to come home to a place like this.

Now, even that is lost to me forever.

A silent tear trails down my cheek, but that's all the emotion I allow to leak out. I know how to be tough when I have to be, and right now I have no other options.

"Well, if that's the case, why did my uncle leave? Why did those other people attack me if I'm so important?"

Roxanne waited patiently while my mind whirred, and now runs a hand over her tightly woven braids. "There are some families who have their own interpretation of the spell. They believe that the alpha doesn't *have* to be a Harridan, and that if a new family were to take over, the magic would be bound to them. Because all the blood is so intermingled, you understand. We have several hundred families now, all more or less descended from the same four blood lines with traces of the four from the other pack. Technically, everyone in this town is somehow descended from a Harridan. So the argument is that a full-blooded Harridan doesn't need to be the alpha. Any of her descendants would do... meaning anyone in the pack.

"Because you suddenly became alpha but did not claim your alpha voice, they felt they were in their right to attack you to fight for dominance. However, since all three of them attacked at once, I could declare it an unfair fight and cancel it. I used the beta command to stop them.

"But at the next full moon, they will be prepared to try again."

My hands fly up in frustration. "This is *impossible*. So I'm supposed to take over as alpha when I'm only fucking eighteen and arrived here two weeks ago. I have no idea what to do, and I'm supposed to force people to follow me who don't want to, all for their own good so they don't go crazy and kill themselves? And *why* is this all my problem again?"

"Because you are Lilliana Harridan. I know," she lifts a hand and stops my angry retort, "your name is Layla. But the first-born female of every Harridan is named Lilliana, and despite what your mother raised you as, your legal name is *still* Lilliana. We found your actual birth certificate—did you know you were born in Idaho?—and it lists your legal name as Lilliana Harridan. We didn't know where you went from there. You lived under an assumed name your entire life, but we knew we had reason to hope, and so we kept searching."

I feel so heavy with the weight of responsibility that has been dumped on me. Suffocating under it all. Dying at the ripe old age of eighteen.

I sigh, even the breath in my lungs heavy. "I can feel people, if they are near enough. Is that a wolf thing, or an alpha thing? I could always sort of sense the guys, but now it's everyone." Even now I knew where exactly in the house all twelve of our household staff are. It's kind of eerie, feeling people like homing beacons in the back of my mind.

"That's an alpha thing. Naturally, you were connected to your fated as soon as you crossed onto the pack territory, but sensing everyone is a trait the alpha uses to protect her pack."

"It's too much, too many," the protest comes out a stilted whisper. Those glowing points of warmth are living, breathing people that expect me to protect them. Me, an eighteen-year-old street kid who barely has a GED.

"It's not just you, Layla," Roxanne reaches out and sets her hand on my knee. Through the thick blanket, it's warm, and despite my fury I feel comforted by the gesture. "I'm here, of course. To help you as much as you want. As is everyone in the house, and I'd say at least eighty percent of the pack is completely loyal to you."

"Yeah, it's that other twenty percent I have to win over. Apparently, by a fight, as a wolf?"

"You have us, too." Milo's low voice startles me, and I realize I forgot the guys were in my room while Roxanne and I were talking. They file out now, circling my chair with hopeful expressions.

"How much of that did you guys hear?" I don't know why but I'm suddenly nervous that I said something embarrassing. I got downright petty at one point.

"All of it, but it's nothing we didn't already know," Milo assures me. "We've been waiting for you, preparing to help you guide the pack one day."

"We were *literally* raised for it," Jared adds.

Roxanne stands. "I know I've dumped a lot on you, and I think it's enough for tonight. I'm going to head to bed and leave you with your fated. Perhaps they can answer more of your questions. But if you need me, just shoot me a text." When she leans down to hug me, I accept it stiffly, still not prepared to forgive her. I know she isn't entirely at fault for the way things have been handled, but my trust is shredded to tatters, and the pain of it throbs like a raw wound.

After she leaves and closes the suite door gently, I let my gaze travel among the three guys surrounding me. "So... you guys never had a choice, did you?" My voice is sad and small, tears prickling at my eyes.

Milo and Landon share a look.

"A choice about what?" Jared asks, sounding genuinely curious.

"A choice about *me*. You were told you're my 'fated mates' or whatever and that's why we were all suddenly besties the second I arrived. It has nothing to do with who I am." My chest tightens, heart squeezing at the painful thought. I had so many hopes that ended up dashed on the floor in one fell swoop tonight.

"No, Layla, it has everything to do with who you are," Milo assures me. "Yes, the bond spoke to us immediately—we felt it when you crossed into Smoky Falls territory that first night—but it's not like we don't like or care about you as a person."

Landon clears his throat. "Fated mates are... well, to be honest, they're basically made for each other. We're connected, but more than that, the four of us form a perfect unit. We complement each other, bring out the best in each other and make up where the others lack."

"Yeah, like clearly I have the sense of humor these two lack," Jared jokes, drawing a tiny smile from my lips. "And you like my dumb jokes. Landon and I aren't the best speakers, but Milo always knows how to speak up. And Landon-"

"Plays a mean game of Minecraft?" I supply.

"Ouch, is that all I am to you?" Landon pressed a palm over his chest in mock pain.

"Landon has the biggest heart," Milo says. "He's the one who's always looked out for us, and since you've arrived, he's been especially concerned about your happiness."

"So, where do I fit into all of this?"

"Right in the middle," Jared teases.

I swat him on the shoulder. "No, seriously, aside from my apparently important pedigree, what is my role in this apparently fated quartet?"

"You're the glue that holds the entire world together, Layla," Milo answers softly. "Isn't that enough? I certainly think that's a heavy burden to bear. There is no more important role than that. We exist to support you, to advocate for you, to cheer you up when you're down. You're the one who has to do everything else, and that's enough."

"It's too much," I whisper, chin trembling. "A week ago I was just a girl finally about to experience a normal life. Now I'm supposed to take on the responsibility of this entire pack. Let alone accepting that tonight, I morphed into a giant wolf—I'm saving that one to unpack later." An involuntary shudder ripples through my body as the phantom pain of the shift flashes in my mind.

"I think," Landon says, standing, "That we can save *all* of it to unpack later. I doubt any of us are ready for sleep yet, so why don't we watch a movie or something? Lady's choice."

"A movie sounds great. But I don't want to pick. Just something funny. Maybe nothing supernatural, though."

Jared pops up and grabs the remote. "Funny is my specialty. Why don't you get settled on the couch? We'll assemble some snacks and get a movie queued up."

So that is how I ended up once again pleasantly tucked between Milo and Jared, with Landon's head resting on my crossed legs. I toy with his baby-soft hair absentmindedly, realizing that as wolves I pet both Milo and Jared, but not Landon.

I don't know when it happens, but at some point I drift off to sleep, my head on Milo's shoulder and my blanket-wrapped feet on Jared's lap, fingers resting on Landon's neck.

Unsurprisingly, I do not have another wolf dream.

Chapter Twenty-Two

LAYLA

~

When I wake, I'm tucked into my bed with no memory of how I got here. Mid-morning sunlight streams through my windows, and I feel completely rested. Even so, there's a heavy sense of dread at the back of my mind that my conscious brain hasn't caught up with yet.

I lay for a moment trying to remember, and I hear a low voice just outside my bedroom door. Faint clinks of dishes. The low rumble of the tv.

Milo's out there, I know it immediately. And Jared and Landon. I sense their presence.

And that's when it all rushes back to me.

The nightmare of shifting, the pack, the attack from the other wolves, the story about curses and alphas and bloodlines.

Shit. Well, now I understand the sense of dread.

I think on it more carefully and realize the last I remember is falling asleep on the couch with the guys. They must have carried me to bed in my sleep. I'm kind of embarrassed, but also kind of warmed by the thought. I wonder which one did it, but then I realize it had to be Landon. It just seems like a very Landon thing to do, gently placing me in the bed while they apparently crashed in the suite for the night.

A smile curls my mouth, and I throw back the covers to go check on my 'fated'.

I shouldn't be surprised, but I can't help the laugh that escapes my lips when I open the door. All three hulking boys crowd around my tiny two-seater breakfast table, feasting like starving men. The table's laden with breakfast, including eggs, bacon, sausages, French toast, fruit, and coffee.

They look up simultaneously with guilty expressions despite their stuffed cheeks.

Milo is the first to swallow his mouthful. "Morning, Lex."

Landon holds up a tray covered with a silver dome. "We didn't want to wake you, so we saved you a plate first... but we didn't want to let the rest go cold waiting, either," he adds with a sheepish grin.

Jared glances between the other two and shrugs with a full mouth. "What? I was hungry."

That draws another laugh from me, and I cross into the room. "It's fine. I'm sure Susan made sure there was enough for everyone. Milo, can you pass the coffee, please?" I spot the French press on the table and my desire for caffeine is strong.

By the time I'm settled onto the couch, Landon has arrived to set the tray on my lap and remove the cover. Milo follows with a cup of coffee, generously poured with cream and sugar.

The guys grab their plates and join me, two sitting on the floor and sharing the coffee table while Milo balances his plate on his lap beside me. We enjoy a comfortable breakfast, and it's not until we've cleared the plates and pushed the cart of dishes out into the hall that the weight of everything revealed last night settles over me again.

"So, how are you feeling?" Landon's intuitive eyes settle on mine, and I can't help my snarky response.

"Well, apparently you *know* how I'm feeling, so why don't you tell me?"

"You're anxious," he answers evenly. "Stressed. Overwhelmed."

"Totally hot for all of us," Jared adds with a wag of his eyebrows.

I laugh again. "You're something else. You know, what's funny is when I first met you I thought you were super standoffish, like you didn't want to get to know me at all."

"I told you," Landon chuckles, "Once you get to know him, you won't be able to get him to shut up."

"Yeah," Milo adds. "He looks all cool, mister jock

popular football player, but really he's just a nerd in Homecoming King's clothing."

"You were Homecoming King?" I raise an eyebrow.

"It's not a big deal," Jared's gaze drops, and I swear he'd be blushing if his cheeks weren't already dark. "It's not like Smoky Falls High is a big school. I didn't have much competition."

Milo smacks him on the arm. "Thanks, asshole, we were both in your class, too."

"Like I said, no competition," Jared grins up at me with twinkling eyes.

"Well, I'm just glad you're the one who had to stand next to Amber the whole time, and not me," Landon laughs, and Jared throws a pillow at him.

"Dude, it's not funny! She kept pinching my butt *all* night! I swear my entire cheek was black and blue after that."

Now all of us are rolling in giggles.

"Look, I feel bad for the girl," Landon says with a grin. "I bet she thought it was her lucky night. You were the king, she was the queen, and she was finally gonna get in your jock. Head cheerleader and football star, a match made in heaven."

"Yeah, well, she's delusional. And she *has* a fated, so I don't know why she'd think she could just go after anyone else."

My mood instantly sinks. They brought up wolfy stuff again. "How does that work, exactly? If someone doesn't want their fated, what do they do?"

Milo shrugs. "Well, it's not exactly that simple.

You're not *forced* to be with your fated, but they're your ideal match in every way. Just by hanging out together, most people realize they are head over heels for their fated and they happily end up together." I don't know if this reassurance is aimed particularly at me or not, but a warm, glowing sensation spreads in my chest. *He essentially just said that I'm perfect for him, right?*

But I don't voice those thoughts. Instead, I say, "You said 'most'. What about the others?"

"If they're not totally in love with their fated, they go to a counselor to see if they can make it work. It's always better to be with your fated than not. But for those who just can't do it, they have to find someone without a fated, or if they haven't manifested yet, they can go to the human world and give up their wolf."

"Roxanne made it sound like the Montrose Pack are kind of our enemies, because of the whole curse thing. Is that true? No one's mentioned it, but I'm guessing they aren't the only pack around?"

"Montrose is complicated," Landon explains. "Most of us are distant relatives of people in that pack. Because of the history there, Smoky Falls doesn't allow people from Montrose to come here seeking an un-fated. But my understanding is they are happy to accept defectors on their side."

"What do you mean, defectors?"

"Well, you can't exist as part of two packs. Someone from Smoky Falls couldn't stay in this pack and have a Montrose mate. They'd have to choose one for both of them to join. So it's called defecting, when you leave your pack for another. It's not done very often, because you give up your family, friends; basically everyone and everything you've known."

"But," Jared adds, "You get the chance for a mate and a future, which, if you're un-fated, you're born without. So most people find it a good option. And yes, to answer your question, there are other packs around. Montrose isn't the only option. It's just that people from our pack are more likely to find a compatible mate there."

"Where are they? How far away?"

"They're in North Carolina, a few hours from here by car."

My mind churns that information over, along with my year in LA with Roxanne. "So, it's not everyone who can't leave for more than twenty-four hours because of the curse, right? It's just the alpha?"

Jared shrugs. "Right, and her mates, once they complete the bond."

"Wait, what?"

Milo nods. "Yeah, once the Harridan alpha completes the bond with her mates, they become alphas too, so the curse extends to them."

"So you guys are fated to me, to fall under this curse —even though it doesn't touch you yet—and you're *okay* with that?"

All three nod in unison.

"Yeah, it's our destiny," Landon shrugs. "How can you not be okay with destiny?"

"It helps that you're cute," Jared adds with a wink and a grin.

My eyes roll. "I'm glad you don't find me hideous."

"It's not that, Lex," Milo adds gently. "You're perfect for us, and we were born to complete you. I know you feel it, that sense of *right* around us. We've felt the same around each other since we were kids, and now, with you here, it's *whole*. There was always one piece missing, and you're not missing anymore. You're home."

Tears bite at the backs of my eyes. *Home.* I do feel home.

And I *do* feel connected to these guys. I don't know if I could call it love, or anything close to that at this point. But I feel like they are important, closer to me than anyone I could think of in the world.

"You're right," I sigh. "I do feel connected to you. But I just met you all and I'm still getting to know you," I admit with lowered eyes. "I like you, we're friends, and obviously you're all hot-"

"You heard it, she said I'm hot," Jared's voice is smug.

A loud smack, followed by Milo's voice, "She said we're *all* hot."

A snort escapes my nose, and I glance back up. "BUT, I just met you barely two weeks ago. I came here expecting to be a wallflower for a while, settle in, take some classes and maybe meet a couple people, make a couple friends. This is…" I wave my hands in useless circles.

"Too much," Landon nods sagely. "It's too much, and we understand that. And there's no pressure from us, Layla. We're here to support you, give you whatever you need. I'm not sure if it was obvious or not, but we all think you're cute too." Bright spots of color appear on his cheeks. "But we definitely don't want to rush you. For now, we just want to help you however you need us."

The other two nod earnestly, and the knot of anxiety in my chest eases. "You mean that? There's no freaky wolf-mates clock ticking down to our inevitable mating?"

A guilty look crosses all three of their faces, and Milo answers. "Well, at the next eclipse, you have to declare whether you intend to accept your fated. That's when you can 'officially' officially become alpha, the kind that can't be challenged. Until then, if you don't find your voice, they can challenge you every full moon. We don't have to mate at that point, but you have to accept us as mates in order to seal and renew the magic."

"And when is the next eclipse?" I ask, already panicking at the thought of wolf challenges every full moon.

"Three months."

"Three months?! I have to decide my entire life in the next three months?" The weight of responsibility comes crashing back full force, pressing on my chest, making it nearly impossible to breathe.

"Layla, I hate to put it this way, but your life has already kind of been decided," Landon says in a gentle voice. "You just have to decide to accept it, or not."

"So... for the next three months, every full moon, I can expect to get jumped?"

"I would assume so," Milo agrees darkly. "I think Amber is pretty determined to wrench the status as alpha away while she has the opportunity. Of course, you'll shift every night, and there will be a pack run every night, but you don't have to attend them. Just the full moon ones."

"Who were the other two wolves that attacked me? I assume one was Amber. Was it the other girls? Or the twins from bio?"

"Yeah, it was the Westley twins. One of them is Amber's fated, one of them is un-fated. So I'm guessing they think she's going to become alpha and claim them, but even if she were successful, it wouldn't work that way."

"Why not?"

"Because she'd have to mate with one from each family. Which is why the whole thing is bonkers. She's been after the three of us for years, like she thinks if she makes herself alpha, she'll just take your fated mates... except she's Landon's direct *cousin*. So they're from the same bloodline, and in order to make it equitable, she'd have to have someone from the Harridan bloodline."

"But I'm the only one left. Wait, you said all of our

blood is mingled throughout the pack. Is there another family that's close enough to work?"

"Yeah," Milo answers glumly. "Mine."

"Wait what?" The revulsion creeps into my tone. "How closely are we related?" I take in his dark hair with completely fresh eyes.

"For starters, it's not the same in wolf packs as it is in regular humans, so get those impure thoughts out of your head. There's no negative to cross-breeding as long as we're one generation removed. But our great-grandparents were siblings. Because of the magic, the female Harridan bloodline stays pure, so everyone that is born of a pairing with a Harridan female is full-blooded Harridan. You and your uncle are pure-blooded Harridan.

"My great-grandfather mated a descendant of the Jean-Yves line, my grandfather mated someone who was an even blend of several families (many steps removed) and then my mother mated into the Vernice family, who are descendants of the Willowbrooks. So I'm roughly a quarter full-blooded Harridan, with the rest being too mixed to really count."

"So there's Harridan, Jean-Yves, Willowbrook, and what's the last main line?"

"Baker, that's my family," Jared answers. "I'm roughly a third Baker."

"I'm a little over a quarter Jean-Yves," Landon supplies. "When the fractions get too small and muddy, you just stop counting them, and stick to the purest family line."

My brain swims. "If I'm following—that means that there are families in town named Jean-Yves, Willowbrook, and Baker? And they represent the supposedly 'pure' lines?"

"Pretty much," Milo answers. "You'd be shocked to see the family trees people like Amber have. She's a Jean-Yves, like that's actually her name. They remarry into the family every two generations to keep the bloodline clear. Fortunately, the fated mates seem to help, but the vast majority of the people in town are just a muddy amalgam of all four bloodlines."

"And that's why you three are my fated," I nod slowly, following along. "Because you're all distinctly, traceably, from one line in particular."

"Yep," Jared answers. "The Westley twins are Willowbrook descendants, but less than an eighth. I bet Amber found that offensive. It's hardly enough to get on the family tree. Jeremy, the one that's fated to her, will drop off if they go through with the pairing. Then it'll only be her line that matters. She's a full half Jean-Yves, as both her parents were a quarter."

I scrunch my eyebrows in confusion. "Is that actually how that works? That doesn't add up to me."

Milo shrugs. "I'm not sure I really understand it. It's the seers who track it all, but the trackable lines are all that matter to them. So they claim if she gets a quarter from each side, that totals a half. Honestly, the only ones who really care all that much anymore are the original four families, and it's a non-issue since you're here now. Amber may have thought she stood a chance of waiting out Dom and taking his place, but there's a full-blooded Harridan female in Smoky Falls now." He grins at me with amusement. "She'd better just mate Jeremy and start working on her puppy talk."

"I dunno guys. I have no idea how to handle any of this," I admit. "Roxanne said I don't have my alpha voice, and she thinks I won't get it until the alpha ceremony during the eclipse. I don't know how to fight as a wolf. If they attack me all together again Roxanne can stop it, but she already told me it's a legit fight if it's just one-on-one and she won't be able to intervene. How the hell am I going to keep Amber from killing me and taking my place before the eclipse?"

"Easy," Jared grins. "We're gonna teach you."

Chapter Twenty-Three

LAYLA

~

The next few weeks are pretty bizarre.

During the day, I attend classes with my fated mates. Now that I've shifted, and the wolf is out of the bag, the dividing social lines are even more obvious. No one will do anything overtly threatening, but they mean mug me in the halls, deliberately bumping into me or other kinds of dramatic high school tv show crap. Milo, Jared, and Landon have taken to forming the 'flying V' position, as I call it, with one on either side of me and one behind, typically Landon because he's the tallest. Even though we have yet to set a descriptor to our relationship other than 'fated', for now I often hold hands with one or more of them for support. Landon will throw an arm around my shoulders while we talk, and I just end up spending a lot of time in physical contact with one or more of them.

The electric tingles are reassuring and despite my constant, nagging worry, I still find every single one of them attractive in their own way. I still think Landon looks like a ridiculously tall rock star, and it's even hotter that he's so sweet and considerate. I love talking with Milo, who apparently has read nearly as many books as I have, and love discussing his favorites. I'm growing more and more fond of his hipster style. And Jared is the all-American football-playing jokester who always has a grin and a cheesy joke to make me smile.

At night, however, we take advantage of the one hour to run as wolves, and the guys try to train me at wolf fighting.

Since Jared's done more scrapping—apparently he has a lot of brothers—he remains in human form and tries to instruct me verbally while I face down Milo or Landon. He's a skilled teacher, very patient and instructive.

But I'm a terrible fighter.

Repeatedly, the guys find purchase on the back of my neck, or they flip me on my furry back, and bite gently at my throat. No matter how slowly we run the same scenarios, I always end up losing.

After three weeks, it's beginning to feel hopeless.

"I'm not getting any better," I grumble to my tray in the cafeteria. "I might as well just give up now."

"That's not true, you're loads better than you were three weeks ago," Jared disagrees. "It's difficult, and you're still learning your new body. You're getting better every day."

"Maybe, but I won't be good enough to defeat Amber in a week," I grouse. "There's just no way I can get good enough to take down someone who's been doing this their whole life."

"Who's been doing what their whole life?" Savannah plunks down her tray beside me.

"Amber, fighting as a wolf. She's going to challenge me at the next full moon and I'm nowhere near close enough to fight her."

Savannah raises a brown eyebrow. "Who's training you?"

I gesture listlessly to the guys. "The experts, apparently."

I jump when she throws back her head and laughs, so heartily I swear tears are coming out of her eyes. It's not until she looks around and realizes no one else is laughing that she pauses. "Wait, you're serious?"

I shrug, raising my eyebrows. "Yeah?"

"Oh girl, you need someone else to train you. Like, now," she stabs a forkful of cheesy pasta and shoves it into her mouth.

"Why do you say it like that?" I'm genuinely curious; her matter-of-fact tone is thick with the implication that there's something else I'm missing.

"Shit, I forget you don't know this stuff. Still, I assumed Roxanne would tell you."

Roxanne has tried to speak to me on a number of occasions, but I've blown her off.

Guiltily, I shake my head at Savannah. "I've kind of been giving her the silent treatment."

"Okay, damn. Well, for starters, you don't *want* to fight your mates, so your wolf instincts aren't going to kick in. You don't actually want to hurt them, and neither does your wolf."

"That's fair," I agree, wondering why the guys never mentioned this.

"Second, they're *males*. They know nothing about actual fighting. Yes, I know," she raises a palm and cuts off Jared's angry outburst, "*technically* anyone can become alpha and a wolf fight is a wolf fight. But, female to female, your instincts aren't triggered until you're fighting another female. Because then it *feels* real to your wolf. And then she'll fight back. I'm guessing until this point you've been just trying to tell her what to do, but she doesn't really get into it?"

"Exactly," I breathe, my pulse rising in excitement that I may finally have figured out my problem.

"Yeah," she nods sagely. "You gotta practice with a girl, sweet cheeks. You'll never get better goofing off with them."

"Will you practice with me?" The request blurts from my lips before I even think about it. "You're a girl, one of the few I know, and you don't actually want to kill me. Seems like a win-win."

"Sure," she shrugs, "but you can't hold it against me if my wolf takes a little fur. You're new and she loves to fight."

"Deal," I agree quickly. "Meet at my place tonight?

You can come up at midnight, or you could come for dinner and hang out?"

"Hell yeah, girl time! I bet you haven't gotten much of that lately."

"I can't say I've had much of it, ever," I confess, heat rising to my cheeks. "My mom died when I was fourteen and since that…"

Savannah's eyes go as round as saucers. "Okay, we're going into full on crisis mode here. I need to pick up a few things, and then we're having a girl's night. Tomorrow's Saturday. Shall we make it a sleepover?"

My panicked eyes rise to the guys, and they all shrug back to me as if to say, *"you're the boss!"*

"Okay, yeah, that sounds like fun. Girl's night."

"Your mates can come up for the shift if they want. They'll probably be anxious." She gives each of them a steely stare. "But just for the shift, understood? You've been hogging her since she arrived, but tonight she's mine."

Landon smiles. "I think it's a great idea. Layla should spend time with people other than us, and frankly, it's kind of embarrassing that we didn't realize why the training wasn't going well."

"Agreed," Milo says.

"Fine," Jared huffs, and points a finger at Savannah. "But no telling her any of the jokes I've told you. I'm only allowed to tell her six a day and I've got an entire book to get through. Speaking of… Layla, why can't you hear a pterodactyl going to the bathroom?"

I shrug, giggling. "Why?"

"Because the 'p' is silent," he replies with a pearly grin.

Groans erupt around the table, but I chuckle. "Funny. Hey, what did you say about only being allowed to tell me six jokes a day?"

Milo smacks him on the arm, hard. "Dude, the point is she wasn't supposed to know."

Looking sheepish, Jared explains, "I promised the guys I would limit myself to six jokes a day, so I don't overwhelm you with them. Also, it forces me to have actual conversations instead of just telling strings of jokes."

"Do you actually know that many?" I ask, amazed.

"I do," he answers proudly. "One time I went three hours straight in a joke-off and the other guy eventually gave up. The winning joke was-"

"For another time," Milo interrupts. "That was number four for the day. You only have two left and we're just at lunch."

"You're right, better save 'em for the opportune time," Jared agrees, grinning.

"Another time then, Layla."

"Another time," I agree.

"And I promise I won't tell her any of your jokes, not that I would have anyway," Savannah snorts.

"Okay, cool well if I don't see you before then, see you at my house at seven?" Excitement bubbles in my chest. I've never had a sleepover before. Mom didn't allow people to stay in our house ever, and I could count on one hand the number of times I'd even had a friend over to play, period.

"Perfect," Savannah grins. "Get ready for a killer girl's night!"

∼

Layla

∼

With only movies to go on, I assumed a slumber party was going to be nail painting, hair braiding, and gossiping about boys.

Savannah shows up lugging her PlayStation and an entire suitcase of stuff I don't even want to guess at.

"Are you moving in?" I ask with a laugh, helping to haul the heavy case to the elevator. I shooed Carson off, worried he'd put his back out trying to lift it.

"Funny," Savannah says drily. "Nah, I just like to have all my stuff, and I wasn't sure if you'd want to camp out or sleep in your bed, so I brought my sleeping bag just in case."

"Oh. I didn't think about it. I mean, we have plenty of guest rooms if you want your own bed?"

"Nah, the whole fun is being in the room together." She pants, closing the elevator gate and hitting the button to go up. "I don't mind sleeping on the floor. It's fine."

"Well, I will too. I'm sure there's a sleeping bag

around here somewhere, and we can push the furniture around in the suite to make room."

"Excellent, because there's a guy on Call of Duty that I *sort* of promised to meet up with for a death match." She grins sheepishly. "I hope that's okay. I planned it last night and kind of forgot about it when I was talking about coming over at lunch."

"No, it's cool. I've never played before, so I don't know anything about it."

"Oh, it's so fun. We'll make you a profile and give you the chance to run around and try it out. Basically, you can log in online and play with other people, either as teams or one-on-one, and you're trying to shoot other people. Basically."

"That's… the whole point of the game? Shooting other people?" We exit the elevator and start hauling her stuff down the long hallway.

"Well, there's a lot of different play modes, but in most of them you win by shooting other people to get your objective. There's a lot of different options."

"And you're… into this game?" I glance curiously at her, taking in her twin brown braids and bright blue eyes.

"Oh yeah, I've been playing this game—well, different versions of it—since my brother got his first PS3. Most people don't believe I'm a girl because they expect girls to suck. Then they hear me taunting them after I sniper their asses. It's a blast."

Something tells me this will not be up my alley, but I

dutifully help set up her console and get the system hooked up to Wi-Fi.

I told the kitchen I was hosting a sleepover for a friend, and the ladies were almost beside themselves to make us special food for the occasion. We had barely moved aside the coffee table and cleared a space in front of the tv before Mary and Mrs. Dowling bustles in with a pile of comforters and pillows.

"We can do that." Savannah and I hustle forward to help, but Mrs. Dowling sniffs. "I should think not. Daphne will be in shortly with your dinner, and we'll be finished."

Feeling as if I've just gotten scolded for offering to help, I exchange a quick glance with Savannah, who grins and shrugs, and we step aside to wait while they spread the blankets on the floor.

She isn't kidding—they are lightning efficient. In just a few minutes we have a massive nest of comforters and pillows laid out in the main suite living space, directly in front of the tv, and Mary gets to work starting a fire. Mrs. Dowling carries in a small, low table, and Daphne shows up right on time with the serving cart of food.

As soon as she opens the door, the distinct aroma of hot bubbling cheese and spice of pepperoni hits my nose. It looks like something from a pizzeria, not your basic make-at-home deal, complete with garlic bread, wings, and several bowls of chips and snacks.

"Thank you." I beam at them. "And tell William and

Susan they've outdone themselves. This looks amazing."

Mrs. Dowling's lips purse in her tiny approximation of a smile. "Chef will be pleased. He's been dying for an excuse to use his brick pizza oven out back. We've stocked your fridge with drinks and added extra sweets to your cupboard, but if you want anything else, just let us know. Susan would be happy to whip up a dessert. Roxanne thought you might prefer something more casual."

"This is *perfect*. Thank you so much for everything. It's more than I can ask for."

Her lips spread into a genuine smile. "We're just so pleased that you're here, and settling in. It's good to see you having friends over, and they're always welcome." Her eyes sparkle for a moment, and then, as if remembering herself, she straightens and barks at a grinning Mary and Daphne to leave.

When the door shuts behind them, my head turns to Savannah, who gapes openly at me and the feast that just sprung up around us. "I have to say, I've been here a few times for parties, so I thought I knew the staff pretty well. I have *never* seen Mrs. Dowling smile, ever. She must have a soft spot for you. And this," she gestures, "wow."

"I know." My cheeks hurt from grinning. "I told them you were coming for a sleepover and just asked if we could have dinner in my room, since my uncle is away it seemed like a chance to give them the night off of the formality. I figured they'd bring up a couple plates of whatever was on the menu for the night. I didn't expect them to prepare us an entirely separate meal."

Savannah settles onto a cushion at the table. "A meal that's getting cold. Come on, let's eat and I'll show you the ropes on Modern Warfare."

We scarf down a few slices and then push the table aside so we have a clear space in front of the tv. Savannah walks me through setting up a character and how to use the remote, and although I'm clumsy and terrible, it is pretty fun.

It's even more fun, however, to watch her battle this mystery opponent of hers. His handle is WolfMan0690, and she knows his name is Brandon and he lives in Oregon, but that's pretty much it. She wasn't kidding. They literally run around killing each other as many times as they can before the clock runs out, and she plugs in a second headset so I can listen in as they trash talk. Wolf Man is good, but she's clearly better and he knows it.

While she's kicking butt, the guys arrive and help themselves to our buffet of leftovers, watching Savannah dominate Wolf Man with wide eyes. Their commentary is hilarious, filled with, "oh, daaaaamn!" and "ouch!" and *"brutal*, did you see that?" The obvious respect in their tones tells me she's every bit as good as I think, and it's not just my inexperience speaking.

When she finally signs off, it's to a round of applause and crowing from the peanut gallery on the couch. Savannah stands and takes a few mock bows before she snatches the last slice of pizza from the tray.

Checking my phone, I see it's almost midnight. "I think we ought to head down soon, so we can take advantage of the full hour for training."

Savannah wolfs down the last few bites of her pizza, gesturing toward the door. "Yeah, let's go. I'm excited to see what you've got!"

"Not much," I answer, trailing behind. The guys are excited, already halfway to the stairs.

"I told you, that was more about them than you," she winks. "You'll see."

Chapter Twenty-Four

LAYLA

~

Going outside, stripping my clothes off—with the guys all facing in the opposite direction—and surviving through the pain of the shift is all second nature now. The entire process goes pretty quickly, and I just have to grit my teeth and hold on for the few seconds the change takes.

The first thing I notice that's different is my hackles are up as soon as I'm completely wolf. Nose twitching, my head turns, seeking the source of my discomfort.

There, to my right, is another wolf. A female wolf. My human brain knows it's Savannah, but my wolf self immediately labels her a threat. We're not among the pack, it's just her and I, and I have to protect my mates behind me.

Her feet are splayed, and she's staring me down with gleaming blue eyes.

I turn and mimic her position, a low growl rumbling in my throat. I'm ready for the attack.

"Easy now, Layla." Jared steps up beside me.

What is he doing? He's supposed to stay behind, so I can protect him.

My lips curl and I snarl a warning, stepping past him and glaring over my shoulder. That ought to be a clear enough message.

"Layla, we're here to help you learn to fight, remember? Savannah is your friend. She's not a threat, and she won't hurt any of us. She's just here to help you."

As if to reiterate, the other wolf sits and paws at the air in a friendly gesture, no menace in her posture.

I straighten slightly, my lips falling, but the growl rumbling from my chest doesn't stop.

"I dunno, Savannah, this might not be a good idea. Her instincts have definitely taken over. There's hardly any Layla going on in there."

Immediately insulted that he's implying I'm some kind of wild animal, I bark at him sharply. I haven't gone *feral*. I just know the truth now. These mates are *mine* to defend, and as long as she doesn't threaten them, I'm no danger to her.

Milo and Landon laugh behind me. "I don't think she appreciated that comment, man," Landon says. "She doesn't feel out of control, but she definitely feels more... *wild*. Do you feel it?"

"Yeah," Milo agrees. "There's more of her wolf there than I've felt before. Even at her manifestation."

"I think Savannah is on the money with this one. Maybe you ought to just step back and let them get at it." Landon's advice is sage.

"But what if she gets hurt?" Jared's voice is thick with concern, and the human part of me finds it touching.

The wolf part just wants him to get the hell out of my way.

"She'll be fine. They aren't going to kill each other. A few nicks are nothing, and she'll heal by morning."

Sighing, Jared takes a step forward and meets my gaze. "If this is what it takes, then do it. Just don't forget who the real enemy is, okay? This is just *practice*. Savannah is your friend. Don't lose sight of that." He reaches out as if to run a hand over my head, but I snap at his fingers and he backs up with a surprised expression.

Now my mates are safely behind me, and the other wolf resumes her aggressive stance.

I crouch low and invite her to make her move.

Jared

My heart is beating a mile a minute. It's taking all the strength I have to sit back and let Layla face down another wolf, a wolf who isn't one of us. I knew Milo and Landon wouldn't hurt her, and perhaps that was the problem: she knew it, too.

But here, with another young female, tension is thick in the air like electricity before a storm. Landon is a live wire of nerves beside me, jiggling on his toes, and Milo is the opposite, standing stock still with his arms crossed over his chest.

I'm resisting the urge to throw myself in front of her, so I settle for pacing.

The wolves face each other, a low, steady growl like a hum between them. Layla is snowy white. Unsurprising, since it's a Harridan trait, but different from her uncle because she's completely white, not a drop of color in any of her fur. The startling green of her eyes as a human is slightly more yellow as a wolf, but even from a hundred yards away she'd be impossible to mistake.

Savannah's wolf I've seen before, although I didn't know it was her. She's a light tan, with a darker saddle pattern on her back and dark around the ears. She's slightly smaller than Layla—the more pure-blooded the wolf, the larger they are—and I can tell she's very agile.

Savannah bounces around for a few moments, testing, teasing Layla, watching her reactions. Layla tracks her, paws spread and body low, shuffling to keep the brown wolf directly in front of her.

Without warning, Layla bursts forward in a full frontal attack. Of course, this is what Savannah was trying to provoke, and she darts to the side, spinning quickly to return fire.

They're in it now, grappling and clawing, their bodies clashing together as snarls rip from their canine snouts. Layla is the aggressor, and Savannah seems to be mainly on the defense. I don't know if that is her usual strategy—she seems to be the aggressive type to me—but I can definitely see that she was correct: this wolf differs greatly from the one we've been attempting to teach the last few weeks. She snarls and growls, attacks with teeth and claws, and at one point gets a mouthful of brown fur on Savannah's shoulder.

It's been an intense fight, but they're both obviously petering out on energy. Real wolf fights are abrupt and vicious, only lasting a few minutes. It's not a game of patience and perseverence, it's a game of dominance.

Milo clearly sees what I do, stepping off the porch with his hands raised, walking between the two wolves who've separated and are circling each other warily. "That was an excellent first battle, but I think it's time to call it for the night. Why don't you guys take a couple minutes to recover—you heal faster as a wolf—and then when you're ready we'll turn around so you can shift back."

Layla gives an acknowledging huff, and Savannah drags her paws as she walks further out into the lawn, proving she means no harm, before she collapses on the grass. Her side rises and falls dramatically as she pants, tongue lolling onto the ground.

Layla doesn't seem to be as winded. There are a few red splotches in her fur, but she's far less out of breath than Savannah. She settles on the grass, tucking her feet below her, and takes a position between us and the brown wolf with her nose pointed toward her opponent like she's still on guard. We wait as the wolves catch their breath, allowing their natural healing to take over.

My phone buzzes in my pocket. "Guys, it's five to one. You've got to shift back now." As one, Landon, Milo and I turn to face the house, and I cringe, listening to the painful noises the girls make as they shift back into human form. It's a factor of life, and it never bothered me before, but now any sound my mate makes that isn't pleasurable lights a flame in my chest. She should only ever feel pleasure.

When the girls are talking happily, we feel confident to turn around, and find them mostly dressed and hugging, going over details of the fight while they're still barefoot on the lawn.

"Hey crazies, why don't you come inside and get warm? You'll get sick standing out there in the cold." Landon's tone reminds me so much of my mother I emit a snort.

"What?" he turns on me, defensive. "It's cold, and they're in tank tops and cotton pajama pants. You won't be laughing when Layla comes down with the flu and you're miserable on her behalf."

"You don't get the flu from being outside," Milo laughs. "You really need to ease off the mother hen routine."

Despite our teasing, Layla doesn't seem to mind. She and Savannah traipse back up the stairs, and she's positively beaming, her pale cheeks flushed and eyes glowing. "That was awesome! I finally *felt* her, deep in here," she presses on her chest. "I felt her come out, take over. It was like I was still me, but I was half her, too. Does that make sense?"

The grin spreads across my cheeks. "It makes perfect sense, gorgeous. You're a magnificent wolf. I knew you had those instincts in there."

"Yeah, leave it to Savannah to drag them out. But it makes sense. I didn't want to hurt you guys, let alone fight you. You weren't a threat, so my wolf refused to surface. I didn't understand the shift and the wolf are two separate things."

Truthfully, for me they'd never been two separate things, which is why we had no idea what was happening in our attempts at training her.

But I certainly wasn't going to tell her that.

"I'm glad we had Savannah to help us figure it out," I reply instead.

"She got a few good swipes in here." Landon has been examining Layla's body for injury, and his voice is concerned as he stares at her shoulder. "We should get those cleaned up so they don't get infected while they heal."

"They're just scratches. I barely feel them." Layla

shrugs him off. "And I heal really fast. I'll be fine. These only took a few weeks to heal up completely, even though I had months of physical therapy to re-strengthen my muscles."

She holds out her arms, displaying the long, silvery scars.

"Woah, where did you get those? I didn't even notice them." Savannah reaches out and grasps her arm lightly, turning it for a better look.

"I normally keep them covered with sleeves," Layla admits. "I was attacked one night, back in LA. Some psycho stabbed me in the chest and cut up my arms when I tried to fight back. I guess they were pretty bad, but I was out cold for over a week and by the time I woke up, I was half-healed."

"My gosh, I'm so sorry! That must have been terrifying."

The girls grab the rest of their stuff, and we follow them into the house.

"Honestly, I don't remember too much about it. I remember being jumped and feeling the pain in my chest, but then I passed out and woke up eight days later. I was in pain, but it was already a lot better. Relearning how to move my hands and everything was hard, but I did it."

Landon was quiet after Layla brushed off his suggestion to treat the scratches on her back, but now that we were back in the well-lit house, he spoke up.

"Hey, Layla? Stop for a second."

She pauses, curious, and he approaches to lift her

arm and twist it gently from the left to the right, looking closely at the silvery scars. With one more glance at the fresh claw marks on her back, his voice turns grim.

"I don't think those are cuts, Layla. They look like claw marks. I could be wrong, but it looks to me like you were attacked by a wolf back in LA."

Chapter Twenty-Five

LAYLA

~

"There's no way. I remember a man. And the report said my friends saw a man with a silver knife or something." My arms cross over my chest, and I stare at the four of them in disbelief. "Besides, no wolves knew where I was. They didn't figure it out until my uncle saw my picture on the news *after* the attack."

"And everyone believed those were cuts? The doctors, the nurses, everyone?"

I hesitate; to my knowledge, the only people who saw my arms after they moved me, mid-coma, to Cedars-Sinai, were Roxanne and Dr. Rosen, who were sent by the pack.

My eyebrows lower. "We need to talk to Roxanne."

I whip out my phone and forgo texting, hitting the call button. She picks it up immediately. She's out of breath, obviously walking. "Hello, Layla? Is everything okay?"

"Yeah, I need to talk to you about something. Are you near the house?"

"Yep, I'm just walking back from tonight's run. I'll meet you in the library in ten?"

"Perfect."

I hang up without saying goodbye, then explain to my friends. "Roxanne and Dr. Rosen were the only two people who ever took the bandages off at the hospital. I was moved from the ER in North Hollywood as soon as Dom claimed me, put up in a private room. I don't know what kind of deal he struck to allow them to treat me instead of the hospital staff, but of course Roxanne was using her beta command on me to keep me docile."

"Damn, and you had no idea?" Jared looks guilty, even though it's not his fault.

"I didn't know anything about wolves or alpha voices or compulsion. I just knew it was suddenly very important to me to do whatever she told me, to make her happy and obey. I chalked it up to the fact that she was nice and she was taking me off the streets, healing me, and taking me to start a new life. It's natural to be grateful for that, I'm sure. But I was always upset that I couldn't find it in myself to disobey her and go visit my street family. We were really close, and there was one guy who protected me for a long time. He's the one who found me and called the ambulance when I got attacked. I never got the chance to thank him." I sniff back the stinging tears; it *still* bothers me to think about it. There's no doubt in my mind that Derrek saved my life on the street a thousand times over. I never would have survived intact without him.

"Anyway, let's head up to the library and see what she has to say for herself."

We take the stairs up since there's too many of us to fit in the elevator. By the time we reach the top, the scratches on my back don't even sting any more, and I realize I heal even faster now that I'm here on pack lands.

Of course, there's already a fire blazing in the library, and we're only waiting a few minutes before Roxanne shows up.

Her eyes widen when she sees the group I've assembled. "Oh, I didn't realize everyone was here." She passes a hand over her neat braids, woven into a long plait down her back, then straightens her shoulders and marches in.

I'm crammed on the sofa with Savannah on one side and Landon on the other, Milo on Landon's side. Jared has taken a seat in a chair, leaving one spot for Roxanne, which she claims smoothly.

"You had something you wanted to talk about, Layla?" Her voice is even, dark eyes glassy in the firelight.

"I have a few things I want to talk about, actually. I

know, but I think I need to hear you say it. Maybe it will make me feel better."

"Okay, I have nothing to hide from you anymore," her kind smile spreads across her lips, the one that kept me feeling like I had gained a new mother figure for that long year in LA.

The one that I now feel I can't trust.

My throat is sticky with emotion, and I cough to clear it. "When I first met you in the hospital, and throughout the time in LA, I had a strange compulsion to listen to you, to trust you, to do what you said. Was that you using your beta voice on me?"

She nods. "Yes, it was. I'm sorry, Layla, but your uncle commanded me to make sure you came back to Smoky Falls with whatever means necessary."

"But *why* was that necessary? You didn't even try to trust me! You didn't give me a chance. I was still wrapped in bandages, hooked up to machines, when you started!"

"I could see in your eyes that you would have run at the first opportunity. I couldn't take that chance. You were too important. You know now why we had to bring you back here. I'm sure you understand that aspect."

My head shakes from side to side. "I feel like you tricked me. I've always followed my instincts, *trusted* my instincts, and by using your beta command on me without me knowing what it was, it feels like you turned my inner voice against me, manipulated it to tell me what you wanted me to think."

"I understand why you feel that way. The only justification I have for myself is that I was doing what I thought was best for the pack, what the alpha ordered me to do. You were a frightened, feral girl who knew nothing about what waited for her here. I needed you to trust me, so you'd give us a chance. I'm sorry. I couldn't wait for that to happen naturally."

"When did you stop?"

"When you boarded the plane for Tennessee. I knew then we'd get you on pack lands and the mission was successful. I had no reason to continue after that." The way she answers is militant, like a soldier giving a report before a commander.

I want my voice to be equally steely, but there's still a note of petulance when I ask, "Why didn't you let me visit my friends, just once? To say goodbye, to thank them for saving me?"

She shifts slightly, her lips pursing, before she answers. "It's complicated, but basically it was a risk I wasn't willing to take. It could have put you in danger again, going back to the place you were attacked. He could have gone back looking for you there, spotted you, and followed you back to our apartment. I couldn't risk it."

It's the truth, but something is telling me it isn't the whole truth.

"Speaking of my attack, I have a question about it."

"Absolutely, I have no more need to deceive you."

"The wounds I sustained: were they from a man, or a wolf? These scars, are they knife marks, or claw marks?" I hold out my arms for emphasis, the long scars reflecting glimmers of light from the fire.

Roxanne sighs. "To be perfectly honest, we weren't sure then and we're still not now. We suspect a bit of both."

"Explain."

"I think you've figured out now that 'Dr. Rosen' isn't just a doctor. She's a witch that sometimes works with our pack. As a shifter, you naturally heal faster than a normal human, but un-manifested and off of pack lands, it's barely consequential. The severity of your injuries was so much that we didn't want to risk it. Your uncle charged Maria and I with accelerating your care.

"From what we could tell, someone definitely stabbed you in the chest with a silver implement."

I can't stop myself from interrupting. "Is silver poisonous to wolves, like silver bullets in movies?"

"No, that's just make believe. But witches often use tools of pure origin—silver, gold, crystals and stones—in their spells. There were a few flecks of silver where the dagger nicked your ribs."

A phantom pain squeezes my chest, and I feel my friend and mates wince around me.

"So you think it was a witch that attacked me?"

"We're not sure. Some of the wounds on your arms seemed to come from something surgically sharp. Others were more jagged and curved, like claw marks. Like you had two attackers, or the person shifted mid attack and kept going. We didn't really know, we just did our best to stabilize you and help you heal quickly."

"So why would someone attack *me*, a random home-less girl on the street, with a witch's knife and perhaps their wolf claws?" It didn't need to be asked, but I still wanted to hear someone say it.

"To our best guess, they knew who you were. Perhaps it was someone from the Montrose Pack? We can't say for certain. We just knew we had to get you out of there and back to the safety of pack lands."

"If it was so urgent to get me back here, I wonder that it took my uncle a year to accomplish it."

Roxanne shifted again. "That was actually my suggestion. I felt it was important for you to arrive healthy, on a same educational level with your peers, and with a few established relationships so you'd feel a sense of trust when you arrived and we could help you through the manifestation. If we'd brought you back here immediately, you would have shifted the first full moon after your attack. You would have been forced to take over the pack at seventeen without even a high school education. Knowing the dynamics that your uncle had been dealing with, I didn't think you were ready to face that challenge. You've grown so much since we first met in that hospital room. I feel like I made the right decision."

Of course she's right. I was in no shape a year ago to deal with what I'm facing now. I'm barely in the right place to *think* about it at this point, let alone going through physical therapy and studying for my GED at the same time.

"I understand." I nod in acknowledgment. "I don't

appreciate the deception, but I can see now you made the best decision you could." With a heavy sigh, I release the resentment in earnest. She might have kept things from me, and manipulated me at points, but I can tell she did it with the full belief that she was making the best possible choice.

"So, what do we do now?" I turn to my friends and advisors.

"Now you keep training to face the challenge on the next full moon. You know Amber Jean-Yves will challenge you. It's imperative that you're prepared."

"Yeah, we're doing that, but if there's someone out there who knew who I was and tried to kill me, now that I've surfaced, they're bound to attack again. For all we know, the person who attacked me is part of this pack, trying to end the Harridan line so their family could take over."

Roxanne scoffs. "That's not likely. Either way, you're safe for now. Preparing for that dominance challenge should be the only thing on your mind."

"Yeah, we're working on it," I growl through my teeth. "That's why Savannah came over. We were fighting during wolf hour. The guys were helping me before, but Savannah said it would work better to fight a female, not my mates, and she was right." I turn to her and smile. "Do you think we can keep this up for the next week?"

She looks a little pale. "I dunno, Lalya, you're untrained but powerful with killer instincts. I-"

"I should train you," Roxanne interrupts.

"Why you?"

"Because I'm your beta. Aside from you, I'm the most powerful female in the pack. I will present a better challenge.

"Plus, if you can defeat me, you will easily defeat Amber Jean-Yves."

Chapter Twenty-Six

LAYLA

~

Once again, I know Roxanne is right. She has tricks up her sleeves that no one else will have, and if I want to turn into an unstoppable alpha in the six days remaining, I need to work with the best.

We agree that I'll train with her the following night and say our goodbyes. I'm still not a hundred percent over all the deception, but I understand it was coming from a place of care for my wellbeing, so I'm trying to let it go.

By now it's so late that I feel bad kicking the guys out. Besides, I enjoy having them here. So Savannah and I give up our nest on the floor for the guys and clamber into my bed together instead.

I drift off thinking how nice it feels to not be alone

anymore. I was always so self-reliant, and now I don't want to be anywhere without my fated. My mind briefly wonders if that's a wolf pack thing too, or I'm just tired of being lonely.

The next morning we enjoy a lazy breakfast before everyone heads back to their respective homes. Every time the guys leave, I'm finding it a little more difficult to watch them go, and I secure their promise to return tonight before I let them leave.

If I thought I wanted back up for fighting Savannah, I know I need it to face Roxanne.

The afternoon passes quickly, and before I know it the guys are turning up just in time for dinner. We hang around the suite until it's time to prepare for the shift.

Roxanne is waiting for me on the lawn, wearing her typical demure uniform of khaki pants and a white button-down shirt with flat ballet shoes. She wore some version of that outfit for the entire year we lived together, lending to the motherly image I have of her in my mind.

Suddenly, I realize it never occurred to me to ask if she has a mate. I'd asked once, back in LA, if she had a family. She'd deflected and said I was her only family.

"You ready for this, Layla?" She asks as I approach.

"Ready as I'll ever be, I suppose," I shrug. "Hey, I realized I don't know. Do you have a mate?"

Her head shakes slowly, swinging her long braids. "No, I was not born with a fated." Her eyes are dark and luminous in the moonlight, and like a lightning bolt, the truth strikes me in my gut. All the signs were there, and I never put two and two together.

"My uncle," I breathe. "You love him."

She gives me a sad smile. "I will say I had hoped that perhaps, once we found you and made sure the pack was taken care of, that he might offer me a place beside him. We worked together as a team for so long, and so few un-fated's are born in this pack. It's almost as if *we* were fated, in a way."

"And he never said anything to you?" Emotion clenches my throat; it's just like a movie, where the boss is so busy with running the company he doesn't realize his VP is in love with him and happens to be his perfect match.

"Not once," she answers with a shrug. "I thought we'd have time to talk after, but no one has seen or heard from him since you manifested. It's almost as if he couldn't wait to leave everything, and every*one*, behind." I don't miss the tremor in her voice on that last painful admission.

"But won't he go mad? I thought that's what you said. Once people have manifested they can't go live among humans anymore."

"Oh, I'm sure it wouldn't be hard for him to find a place with another pack. He has an excellent pedigree," she winks conspiratorially. "He probably already had a place set up, maybe even a mate waiting for him."

"I-" Just as I start speaking, her cellphone alarm goes off.

"Looks like it's time, Layla. Just let your wolf take

over. If you want to use your conscious mind, focus on finding your alpha command voice. If you can issue an alpha command, you can stop me from attacking you. No one will question your legitimacy any longer once you find it."

"And you can't just stop her with your beta voice?" I ask, hopeful even though I know the answer.

"No, there are some rules as ancient as the mountains. The pact the four families made only stands so long as a Harridan is the strongest heir. You have the bloodline, but if your wolf cannot command hers, you are not strong enough to make that claim. She's within her rights to challenge you to prove it, and I do not have the authority to stop it, so long as she challenges you without help."

"Very well. Then let's get this show on the road and see what I've got."

Roxanne reaches out and pulls my shocked body to her in a tight hug. I'm resistant at first, but then I relax and allow my arms to circle her waist, resting my cheek on her shoulder.

Her whisper is warm and sincere. "I'm very proud of you, you know. Your mother would be, too. You're going to make an excellent alpha. You just need to *believe* it."

Tears prick at my eyes and I lean into her heavily, squeezing tighter. While she'd been sort of maternal in LA, we'd been more like siblings. I longed for her approval, but she didn't act like a mother.

This felt different.

"Thank you," I whisper, then pull back. "But don't think that's going to make me go easy on you. My wolf is her own animal. I found that out last night."

Roxanne grins, her smile pearly in the moonlight. "I would expect nothing less from a Lilliana Harridan."

"Yeah, that's never going to feel like my name." I turn my back to her and start pulling my sweater over my head, before I catch sight of the guys, staring. "Hey, turn around, jerks!"

They immediately whip around to face the building, and I take several steps away from Roxanne before I strip off my clothes and call on the shift.

She doesn't make a noise, or if she does, I'm too caught up in my own shift to hear it. Before my change is even complete, I feel the threat, like electricity in the air. Her beta power presses on the surrounding atmosphere, invading my space, making the air close. I snarl, pushing back to create a bubble of space for myself to breathe. It's like her aura is trying to dominate mine, and I'm determined to keep her from winning before we even touch teeth to fur.

Roxanne's wolf is mostly black except for the silver tip of her tail and a matching silvery mask. She glares at me, her dark eyes reflecting silver in the moonlight, snarls ripping from her chest with no hint of restraint.

My wolf snarls back, jaw snapping, and I feel as though my aura-power-dominance has met hers in the middle now. It'll be interesting to see what happens when our bodies collide.

Ever confident, my wolf bows aggressively, shuffling forward across the turf to push into Roxanne's space.

And just as we race forward to meet in the middle, I feel it; her beta voice, pressing at my self-control, trying to command me.

My wolf stumbles, taking a hit and allowing Roxanne to get a mouthful of fur before we recover. Shock ripples through me at first, but then I'm fighting back. Using all of my mental strength, I press back against the onslaught of her command, and my wolf rallies for another attack.

The bodies of the wolves rip and snarl, bite and claw, but the more intense fight is going on in our minds. My wolf has taken over physically, trusting me to protect her from Roxanne's mental attacks. She prods me, threatening to command my wolf to lie down and expose her belly.

I push back angrily, trying to reverse the command and force *her* wolf to obey. It takes everything I have to hold the surrounding bubble and keep us from falling prey to the command voice.

But it's exhausting. Like a muscle I've never used before, my resistance is weak and caving under the pressure. The bubble around us shrinks until it disappears, and Roxanne's voice resonates in my head: *Give up.*

My wolf stops fighting, lying in the ripped up grass and exposing our white belly in submission. In the human corner of my mind, I scream in frustration. She's not supposed to be able to do that! I'm supposed to be some kind of super powerful alpha. Why is a beta bossing me around?

Roxanne accepts our surrender, then trots off to her pile of clothes. I'm not physically hurt, but every step is exhausting. The energy it took to fend off her attack for as long as I did left me depleted both physically and mentally.

Emotionally, I'm also a wreck, which I let her know as soon as we're dressed.

"I can't believe you did that to me! You said you couldn't use that on me anymore."

Roxanne is nonplussed. "I didn't do it to bend you to my will, Layla. I did it to show you what *you* have to do, what you still need to learn. Find your voice and force Amber to submit.

"You may be a stronger fighter than her. You may not be. But your legitimacy is *without question* if you possess the alpha voice. You can limp through the next three months, fending off regular attacks at the full moon, or you can establish yourself as alpha now and set to work bringing the pack back together with that energy instead. Of course, it's up to you, but I know which option I would choose." She wraps an arm around my shoulders and squeezes. "I know that was a lot for the first time, but I can't take it easy on you, because no one else will. There is no space in this world to coddle you, I'm afraid. But I don't really think you need it. You're a Harridan, after all."

We reach my mates, waiting on the porch. "I'll leave you to recover, and let's meet out here tomorrow, same time. There's only five more nights until the full moon."

A heavy sigh pours from my lips, and I nod. Even though I don't feel remotely like going through that again, I know she's right. "Okay, tomorrow."

～

Milo

～

For the next five days, we do everything we can think of to support Layla while she gets her ass handed to her by Roxanne repeatedly. After the first night, Roxanne forces her to battle twice each night. First for as long as she'll go, then again after a brief rest.

Every time ends with Layla on her back in the grass.

The wolves fight and score bites and scratches on each other, but I know the worst part is something we can't even see.

We can hear it; Roxanne's beta voice echoes through our skulls, the same as the alpha's, an odd double-timbre when she commands Layla to give up over and over again.

To us, it's incredible to watch Layla resist. She didn't know she was a wolf a few weeks ago, so to see her resist the beta command is almost absurd.

But she's supposed to be the alpha, and she doesn't have a voice.

Layla explains to us that in her mind, she's doing the same thing. Thinking as hard as she can, trying to command Roxanne to lie in the grass with her belly skyward while their wolves duke it out.

We never hear her voice once.

When I question Roxanne if she shouldn't be teaching Layla physical moves, tricks she can use to dominate an attacker, she scoffs.

"You think her problem is physical? No, physically she can outmatch any wolf in the pack, I promise you. Her wolf will handle herself in a fight.

"Layla's problem is mental. Until she believes in herself, she will fail. Her head will impede her wolf and she will lose. The only way I can think of for her win is for her to accept her status as alpha. When she truly believes it, she will win. When she truly believes it, she will find her voice and then this will be a long-distant memory."

It's painful to watch, but no amount of reassurance from us will convince Layla she is the alpha. She has to believe it for herself, and all we can do is offer support and encouragement every time she finds herself on her back.

"It's hopeless." Layla's near tears. It's Thursday, her last practice before the full moon, and we just witnessed her submit once again to her beta. To be fair, we're all exhausted, and that's wearing on us too. Midnight fights every day of the week, plus early morning classes, added to the stress of the upcoming challenge, would be enough to wear anyone down. We walk back into the house and take the elevator up.

"It's not hopeless." Landon wraps an arm around her shoulders and she leans into him heavily. "You hardly have a scratch on you! Your wolf is kicking butt."

"Yeah, well Roxanne said that doesn't matter if I can't find my alpha voice."

"Look gorgeous, Amber isn't a beta, so she doesn't have a command voice to use on you," Jared points out. "Even if you don't have your command voice, you're much more evenly matched with Amber, and Roxanne even said your wolf is stronger. Even if you don't get your alpha voice, your wolf can still defeat her. You'll be just fine!"

"No, Roxanne's right. I have to prove to everyone, to myself, that I'm the alpha. And right now it's just not there. I don't know if it ever will be. Maybe I'm too late, maybe it's something to do with my mother running away and never manifesting. I don't know. Just... give me a minute. I'm gonna go shower." She trudges into her room, closing the door to her bathroom and leaving the bedroom open.

Lately we've taken to hanging out on her bed. It's easier to stretch out here than on the smallish living room furniture in her suite, which amounts to little more than an oversized love seat and two chairs. On the king-sized bed we can all lounge comfortably, which we do as we wait for Layla to finish getting cleaned up.

"I'm worried about her," Landon admits. "She feels exactly what she said: hopeless."

"I don't know what to do about it." Jared's voice is equally concerned. "She isn't even laughing at my jokes anymore."

"To be fair, your jokes are lame. I don't know why she ever laughed at them in the first place." He glances my way in indignation and I wink to let him know I'm teasing.

"I know, guys, I'm concerned as well. But this is something she has to do for herself. We can't force her into owning her destiny as alpha. We all know it, we've told her, but she's got to believe it for herself."

The door opens and Layla pads out, dark hair piled on her head and a few drips of water marring the light grey of her camisole. It has a matching pair of pink and grey leopard print shorts, and she looks adorably sleepy as she clambers over Landon to slide beneath the covers.

Something about Layla's pajamas is endlessly fascinating to me. She doesn't just sleep in her underwear, like we do. She's got these cute little sets, special clothes for sleeping that are sort of basic, but still sexy with lacy details so they're almost, but not quite, like lingerie.

We all agreed to take our time, be the best friends a girl could ask for, until she has time to settle in as alpha and starts feeling more from our connection. It is inevitable, with the strength our bond already has and how well we get along—she will get there too, in time.

That doesn't help my eighteen-year-old wolf

hormones that are screaming at me I'm inches away from my warm, sweet, deliciously curvy mate. Both Landon and Jared shift uncomfortably, pulling at their jeans in much the same way I'm adjusting.

I've thought about the kisses I stole, right before we tossed her into our insane world, more times than I can count. Usually when I'm home, alone, my brain dredges up the memories of her lips on mine, the delicate skin below her ear. The way she moaned when I pulled her mouth to mine. Maybe I rushed her, I'm not sure. In that moment, I was absolutely certain she wanted it every bit as much as I did. Since then, things have been murkier.

Tonight Layla's nervous despite her exhaustion. She peppers us with 'what-ifs', an endless series of pointless questions, and at some point we all drift off without even an attempt to make up a bed on the floor or make the long drive home.

And I sleep more soundly than I ever have before, sharing a bed with my fated mate and the brothers who will some day form our family.

Chapter Twenty-Seven

LAYLA

~

Friday is the longest day of my life. The sense of dread is there the second my eyes pop open, despite the fuzzy feelings in my chest when I realize the guys are all fast asleep around me.

It only gets worse as we muscle through classes. Surprisingly, I don't see Amber at all, although there are plenty of other people, clearly Team Amber, that fill my day with dirty looks.

The guys head back to the house with me right after school, attempting to distract me during the long hours until midnight. Even the household staff are in on it, apparently. William makes pizza tonight, and dinner has a festive party atmosphere as opposed to a more formal dinner, with everyone taking the night off.

They're all excited, confident that I will put down Amber's challenge and finally take my place as alpha.

I wish I felt the same.

It's been a wild ride, from discovering I had family I didn't know existed, to moving to Smoky Falls, finding out I shift into a wolf, have fated mates, and am destined to take over as alpha to protect every person who lives in this town. Not to mention the curse.

A lot to take in.

But even though a big part of me still feels like an outsider, something deep within my heart of hearts knows this is where I belong. I felt it as soon as I crossed into the pack territory, even though I didn't know what it was at the time. I felt it when I met the guys, my 'fated', and with each new person or experience, I feel myself woven tighter into the fabric of this place.

Even so, I don't feel ready for this challenge. It's one thing to grow up knowing you're meant to lead an entire community, preparing for it your entire life.

It's another to have it thrust upon you, and be told you have weeks to prove yourself. I feel as if that's a total recipe for failure, and the dark resentment swirls in my chest despite the surrounding celebration.

I resent my uncle for bringing me here without telling me anything about who I am or what this place represents. What this town expects of me. And then just taking off into the shadows, never to be heard from again. I thought I'd found my family, only to be ditched as soon as he shunted his curse off on me.

And I resent my parents, who ran away from this

place, raising me to be completely ignorant of who they really were and where I truly belong. On some level I get it, mom was seventeen and didn't want to live her life cursed to stay in a small town in Tennessee forever. They were escaping the curse; I get that.

But to deny me the knowledge of who I am, who my family really is, is an entirely different kind of cruel. Because she had to have known that eventually it would catch up to me. She even named me after herself, giving me the Harridan name, instead of my father's last name or a total alias. Somewhere deep inside, she expected me to come back here.

Mostly, I resent that she ran away at all. It was selfish to leave the running of the pack to her brother, who she knew had no fated mates, no way to extend the line. Did she intend for the entire community to die out when there was no longer a Harridan to helm them? She had to have known the story Roxanne relayed to me, about the magic and the importance of the Harridan bloodline. It seems the ultimate selfish act to value your own freedom over the lives of thousands of others.

Sighing, I glance around at the party once more. These people are counting on me. They're all happy, relieved that I am here to save them.

And I'm going to let every one of them down.

Landon

~

Layla is a roil of emotions, and I have no idea how to comfort her.

From what I can tell, she doesn't really want to be comforted. She's stewing in her thoughts as an escape from her nerves, and I don't know which is worse.

After dinner we retreat to her suite and we do our best to distract her with movies, games, and Jared's terrible jokes, but the raw edge of her anger doesn't dissipate.

Finally, I have to ask. "Layla, are you mad at us for any reason?"

Her green eyes whip to my face, an angry bark her reply. "No, why would you even say that?"

"Because I can sense you're angry, and despite our best efforts to cheer you up, you're still livid. So I wondered if it is any of us you're angry at."

She sighs, uncrossing her arms and rubbing her small hands over her face. "I'm sorry. I'm not mad at you guys. I'm mad at this situation. I'm angry at my uncle for ditching me here and taking off. I'm furious at my parents for setting me up to this impending failure. But I'm not mad at you."

"It's not an impending failure," Jared rubs the back of her neck. "You're going to kick Amber's butt, I know it. You're better than her in every way, gorgeous. Everyone knows it."

"Apparently not Amber," she huffs. "If she did, she wouldn't even try."

"Well, she hasn't seen you training every night," Milo answers reasonably. "And she's grown up with no competition; the assumption that she would take over ran rampant in her family for all those years your mom was gone. I can only imagine they told her every day she would be alpha. That sort of conditioning would be hard to shake."

"So if I lose, then what happens?"

"Number one, that won't happen," Milo is quick to reply. "But if for some bizarre reason it does, then Amber has the assumed position of alpha until she can find her voice. Of course, she would be open to the monthly full moon challenges the same as you if she can't command. But she would be presumed alpha so..." his voice trails off as if he suddenly realizes what he was about to say.

"So what?"

Milo sighs. "So she would move in here with her family. Technically, this is the pack alpha residence, even though it's named Harridan House. By tradition, it would pass to the next alpha."

"Wait, are you saying I'd be homeless? Again?!" Layla's voice rises in panic, and my heart clenches. Somehow, her emotions affect me more strongly than my own.

"Absolutely not," I assure her. "We wouldn't let that happen, and you have a family inheritance. Roxanne has access to your accounts and could get you set up in a place. But you'd have to vacate this house."

Her lower lip trembles, and it takes all of my

restraint to stop myself from grabbing her and stopping it with a kiss. "But this is my *home*. I finally, *finally* got here, and I'm about to lose it."

"Not happening," Jared says confidently. "I think we should stop talking about what-ifs. They will not happen and all we're doing is stressing her out more. Layla is going to shift, kick Amber's butt, then lead the pack on the midnight run. Then we're all going to come back here and get a great night's sleep. Speaking of— Layla, do you want to nap before the run?"

She shakes her head. "There's no way, I'm too nervous."

"Okay, then let's just do a movie. What about New Moon?"

Milo and I groan in unison. "Not *again*, Jared."

"Hey, I just love watching the vampires get their asses kicked by the wolves. Sue me."

Layla chuckles. "Do you guys watch that a lot?"

"Not recently, thank god," Milo snorts. "Jared was obsessed for a while, but we convinced him it was better for his social health if he found something else."

"Social health?" She glances between us, confused.

"Milo said he'd show the cheerleading squad video of Jared watching it if he kept making *us* watch it." I grin widely, remembering.

She laughs. "Wow, you guys don't mess around."

"He was obsessed. It was pathetic."

"Hey it's not pathetic to like something. Don't box me in with your gender stereotypes." Jared crosses his arms and sticks his nose in the air.

"It's not about gender stereotypes," Milo disagrees. "You always wanted to act out the scenes like some kind of LARPer with the movie in the background. It was fucking weird."

Now Layla is full on giggling. "Okay, now I *have* to see it."

"See what you did?" I shoot Milo an accusing glare, but I don't really mean it. The storm cloud of Layla's emotions has settled, and if that means we have to watch sparkly vampires, I'll pay that price.

"Whatever Layla wants, Layla gets..." Jared sings, winking.

"The song is Lola," she corrects him, but her smile is hard to mistake.

"Nah, I think it's Layla," Milo disagrees with a grin.

"Fine. Are we gonna watch this movie or not?"

∾

Layla

∾

Milo and Landon weren't kidding. Watching Jared watch New Moon is a show unto itself. I'm so distracted I don't notice time passing until Milo's phone buzzes in his pocket.

"I hate to break up the party, but it's time, guys."

He doesn't have to clarify. We all know what that means.

317

We make our way out of the suite and down the stairs, my heart going double time.

Unlike the last full moon, the entire household is waiting to join us, including Roxanne. She smiles encouragingly, hugging me with a whisper of 'you've got this!' before allowing me to continue with my fated.

The guys flank me, and the household follows in solidarity as we march through the property, past the gardens, and into the clearing in the woods. As we approach, more and more people join, allowing us to pass through and filling in behind our growing party.

This time is so different from last, when there was just one sea of people all moving toward the same spot. Now there are two obvious heads, me arriving from the direction of the house with thousands swelling behind me.

And Amber, already waiting in the circle when I arrive.

Her faction has already gathered, and they've claimed the far side of the circle from Harridan House.

Once we're all assembled, I step into the circle, reciting the brief announcement Roxanne had me prepare.

"For those who have not met me, I am Lilliana Harridan." My voice trembles lightly, and I clear my throat before I continue in a firmer voice. "I prefer to be called Layla, but in the Harridan tradition I was named after my mother. Before the pack shifts and goes for our run, I have to ask if there are any new manifestations tonight? If so, please step forward."

My stomach is absolutely sick with nerves, but I stand my ground and look around. No one comes forward.

"Very well. The pack run can begin as soon as midnight hits."

"No." Amber steps forward, her blue eyes flashing. "As Layla is not a fully inducted alpha, I claim my right to challenge for the position." She's dressed in simple sweats, an altogether unimpressive challenger as a skinny girl of average height, but I know it's not the girl I will be fighting.

Even though I knew this was coming, it still sticks a knife in my gut.

Roxanne steps forward and nods. "Very well. When the clock strikes midnight, there will be an alpha challenge between Amber Jean-Yves and Layla Harridan. The winner will lead the pack for the monthly run."

And now there's nothing left to do but wait. The guys crowd around me, Landon holding my bag of clothes—I still refuse to strip naked in front of five thousand people—and their closeness helps me breathe more deeply.

There's nothing to do but wait now. My senses are almost overwhelmed with feeling every soul of the surrounding pack. I don't know most of the individual people, but I can sense their individual wolves. It's crazy. I didn't notice it last time, but then again, there was a lot going on that night.

Milo squeezes my hand, and Landon rubs circles on my neck with his thumb, their comforting electric

tingles coursing over my skin. I try to soak in their positivity, their encouragement, thinking over their words
of the last several weeks. A small amount of unease
lives within all three of them, but more than that, they
are confidently positive. I try to let that confidence
bolster me, even though it feels false to claim as
my own.

Suddenly, just like before, a cacophony of cell phone
noise erupts, signaling the change from 11:59 to
midnight.

I'm out of time.

Chapter Twenty-Eight

LAYLA

~

Not wanting to waste any time, I call on the shift and drop to all fours immediately, suddenly regretting my choice to destroy my clothes rather than whip them off and change. Since I've been undressing for the last month it feels strange, but it happens so quickly I don't take time to dwell on the pressure sensation of the restricting fabric before it's torn free.

Of course, no one else has shifted aside from Amber. We are now two wolves in a ring of humans, watching our challenge, waiting for the result.

My wolf is furious that this girl would dare to challenge us. *Doesn't she know her place?* But it's not my wolf who's lacking command, it's me. If I had the alpha voice, this wouldn't be necessary, but here we are.

After my fights with Roxanne, I know how to pull my mind back from blocking my wolf, so she has full control of the fight. But since I'm not fending off mental attacks, I have nothing else to do with my consciousness but observe.

My wolf rumbles low in her chest, sitting primly on her haunches but issuing a warning. *Stop now while you still can.*

Amber's wolf will have none of it. She's mottled in color, her belly and the inside of her legs white but transitioning to tan on her legs and back, with splotches of grey mixed in. She snarls aggressively, single-minded focus clear in her pale blue eyes.

My wolf issues another warning, louder this time, with a snap of her teeth for emphasis. But she refuses to react to Amber's threatening stance. There is no challenge until she physically attacks us, and so we wait.

When she charges, we deftly jump aside, and the fight begins in earnest. As a wolf, I am bigger and stronger than Amber, but not by much. And she's quick; she darts around us, turning on a dime, seeking a soft spot to bite over and over without a second's rest.

It's almost as if she's trying to make us dizzy, confuse us about which way she's going, so we leave a flank unprotected for her to attack.

My wolf is sharp, her eyes tracking Amber's every twist and feint. She does an excellent job of intercepting Amber's constant probes, light on her feet as she shifts and twists our body.

Suddenly deciding she's tired of being on the

defensive, my wolf goes after Amber aggressively. I hear the random cheering and reaction of the crowd, noises when Amber appears to have the upper hand and much more noise when I repel her attacks. The fight seems to drag on forever, every handful of seconds a lifetime as my brain tries to keep up with the fight.

I need to call up my alpha voice and end this, I think helplessly. *But how can I find an alpha voice when I'm no alpha?*

A sharp, piercing pain in my flank brings my thoughts whipping back to the fight. As if proving that I'm not cut out for it, Amber snuck beneath my wolf's defenses and sunk her teeth into our flesh.

My wolf snarls, striking back while Amber prances away with a self-satisfied cough. As she grows more confident, so do I.

Confident I'm going to lose.

I don't know what I'm doing. I don't have the skill, the training, the *experience* to do this. To do any of it. I'm basically some girl who was pulled off the street and thrust into a world I know nothing about, told to sink or swim, and oh by the way, the entire pack is depending on me to win or they could all die.

No pressure.

Angry snarls rip from my wolf's chest as she attacks, leaping onto Amber's back and getting a mouthful of fur, but no flesh, for her troubles. Amber slips out from beneath us and whips around, nipping at our foreleg with sharp teeth.

Pain lances across our leg and my wolf yelps, limping a few steps away before resuming her growls.

There's no question now. I'm losing and everyone knows it. Most of the crowd have gone silent, only a small vocal minority cheering for Amber. Her fur stands on end, trying to make herself look bigger as she stares us down, slavering and snapping her teeth.

This is pointless. There's literally no point. My wolf whimpers as the dire thought bounces around in my brain. Why am I fighting? Maybe it would be better if Amber took over. She's clearly been after the position since birth, training for it. She'd probably be a much better alpha than I would.

As if sensing my weakness, Amber's ice-blue eyes gleam with victory and she pounces, knocking my wolf over. We roll together and I wriggle under her attack, trying to keep from presenting my throat or my soft belly as a target. My wolf kicks out with her hind claws and Amber jumps aside, avoiding the gutting we attempted.

We roll back onto our paws and stand, but the pain has made our body weary. My brain is tired. My wolf is tired. She whimpers softly once more, and I look forlornly at the dirt, considering the cost of laying down, belly up.

"You can do it, Layla!" Landon's voice, strong and clear, pricks up my ears.

"You've got this Lex, don't give up!" Milo's rich, sexy tone chimes in.

"Hey Lex, why did the wolf go into the forest?" My

head turns to catch Jared's beaming grin. "To kick Amber's ass, that's why! Go finish her!"

More shouts rise to join them, a chorus, a *wave* of positivity. The energy hums across my skin and sets my fur tingling.

Chants of 'Alpha! Alpha!' mix with a chorus of 'Layla, Layla!' And something akin to a second wind courses through my body, deadening the pain and weakness, bolstering my resolve.

They believe I can do it. They have lived this life far longer than I. Why shouldn't I believe them when they say they believe in me?

With renewed energy, I charge Amber, who meets my attack with a snarl. Once again, I am the aggressor, my wolf barreling into her body and snapping viciously, deadly intent permeating my mind.

There's no time for 'try'; I have to fight to win, or I've lost before we even began.

I push the attack, rearing up on my hind legs and attempting to rip at the back of her neck. To force her down, force her to obey. Amber scampers out from beneath my paws and spins around, trying to clamp her teeth around my neck from below. She surges forward, flipping me on my back as I scrabble for purchase, pawing desperately to keep her from claiming victory.

It's not looking good. The most I can do is keep her from getting a firm hold, but her teeth are inches from the tender part of my neck and I can't seem to wriggle my way out.

No, I think desperately. *I am so close, I can't lose now.*

All these people are counting on me. They called me alpha. I can do this. I can be the alpha. I have to keep fighting.

My wolf snarls violently, kicking and clawing at Amber who holds a side of our throat in her teeth. Just a few inches to the left and she'll have a firm, end-of-challenge killing grip, and I'll be forced to submit.

I can't let her win.

Deep in my heart, a sudden conviction flames to life.

If Amber wins, the Smoky Falls pack is doomed.

And that will be *my* fault, because I am Layla Harridan.

And I am their alpha.

Heat surges through my chest, a powerful, earth-shattering strength like I've never felt before. My muscles coil and bunch with it, like adrenaline flooding my system and preparing me to take flight.

With a burst of energy, I jump into Amber. She rends a small chunk of flesh from my neck but otherwise loses her grip, and I barrel her over as I regain my feet.

NO.

The command voice reverberates in my chest. I feel the electric sensation pass through my flesh, spreading around me like a ripple in a pool of water. The crowd goes absolutely silent as it hits them.

Amber struggles to stand, and I speak in my alpha voice once more.

Stay down. Submit, and I will release you.

Amber whimpers, then bows her head and crawls forward on her belly, a high-pitched whine emitting from her muzzle. When she's nearly between my front paws, she stops and rolls over, presenting her soft white belly to me in surrender.

My wolf chuffs in acknowledgement, and we step backward.

I accept your surrender. Now go.

Amber scrambles to her feet and runs back toward her supporters with her tail between her legs.

I sit, staring out at the sea of faces I don't recognize, waiting for the next part.

Then I realize they're all waiting for me. When I use the mental strength of my alpha voice, the words flow from me, born on a wave of raw power.

I am Lilliana Harridan, and I am your alpha. Run with me while the moon is full, and renew the magic that bonds us as a pack.

Immediately the crowd cheers, then begins stripping off their clothes and transforming. When I'm attacked by three very familiar wolves with joyful puppy kisses, I know exactly who they are.

Once the pack has shifted, I trot over to wolf-Roxanne with my fated beside me. She tips her snout in the direction of the forest path and I understand. Now I lead with my mates, and she follows behind.

The pack parts for us, and surges in behind. I feel them, every single wolf in a long, winding mass that follows the trail. Some choose to run between the trees, weaving around the trunks like some kind of game.

And now, beyond just feeling their presence, I can get a hint, just a taste, of their emotions. It's almost as if in my mind they have a color, an aura, and I can sense what it means.

And they are all happy. Joyful. Exuberant. There's no anger or resentment or fear; my feelings stretch out to Amber and I sense only relief. She did her part and now no more is expected of her.

Emotion fills my chest; finally, the pieces have fallen into place. I have stepped into my position as alpha; the pack was suffering without a powerful leader, a leader that could promise a future of stability and safety.

Somehow, that leader is an eighteen-year-old runaway from Los Angeles. Go figure.

But the sense of joy, of contentment, that swells in my chest is unmistakable. My fated run directly behind me; they still don't have status as alphas yet, not until we are officially mated. Even so, their joy, their pride in what I've done, is a golden, glowing aura of happiness.

It seems every step I take toward claiming my birthright and reconnecting with my ancestral home, my place in this world, brings us closer together.

And I can only imagine what the future will bring.

Chapter Twenty-Nine

LAYLA

~

It takes the weekend to get everything cleared up and sorted out, but finally we're back on a semi-normal routine.

After the run, we host a smallish celebration among the household staff, friends, and connected families. It feels incredible to have the anxiety off my shoulders, and of course, the guys stay overnight. Truthfully, they stay over every night now, and we've given up the pretense of them camping out in my suite. We share a bed, and their presence sets my soul at ease. I find it harder and harder to be without them.

We have to visit the pack seer the following day, who assures me that my status as alpha is all but declared since I spoke with my alpha voice. Her office is almost a little too on the nose, with a neon palmistry sign and 'Fortunes Read Here' posted proudly in her windows.

Apparently, she makes a good deal of money from visiting tourists to supplement her pack income.

That interesting factoid aside, she advises I won't be 'officially' officially the alpha until we can hold the eclipse ceremony in two months. The alpha voice doesn't actually give me the position, it just makes it impossible for someone to challenge me since I can order them to stand down. Doesn't make much sense to me, but then again, what do I know about wolf customs? As long as things calm down, that's all that matters.

And they do. Now that I can feel and manage the pack, it's a little overwhelming to be so aware of every person in the pack, everywhere, at all times. Roxanne is showing me how to tune out from time to time, which helps. She assures me that claiming my fated at the eclipse will both solidify the magic creating my control and secure the bonds among the entire pack that had been failing for the last two decades.

Which gives me something new to worry about: claiming my fated.

They explain I don't have to actually sleep with them in order to do it, I just have to complete the ceremony that binds us together for eternity and seals the bond.

But that means I have less than two months to decide if I want to tie myself to the three of them and eventually marry them all in the wolf equivalent of a wedding.

That's a little intense for eighteen years old.

Of course I love them. In the short time I've known them, Milo, Jared, and Landon have become the closest friends I've ever had. Derrek notwithstanding, I'd never felt a fraction of the concern from anyone before them. Their every touch, every glance, every word conveys their absolute devotion to me.

And even Derrek hadn't shown me their level of devotion. He was just a guy that protected me and a few dozen other kids on the street, and I worshipped him in the way a teenage girl would.

But it just feels like a heavy decision that I have to make quickly, and the pressure is on.

So as the guys escort me around school, I try to relax but be conscious of every subtle thing they do and how it makes me feel, telling myself that's how I'll measure the possibility of a future together.

And I realize I lean on them more than I knew.

Landon doesn't let me carry my bag anymore, and he always stands behind me, toying with my hair while I literally lean against his chest.

Milo's fingers always seem to be intertwined with mine, guiding me gently through crowds and around obstacles—not that it's really a problem anymore. The angry faces I spotted before the full moon are nowhere to be seen now, and even as I reach out with my feelings, I sense no resentment or anger, just peace among the pack.

Jared has taken it as his personal mission to ensure I never lack for a coffee in the morning, often scribbling jokes on the cup before delivering it to me. I have no idea where we're at in his book of jokes, but something tells me he has plenty more to go before he runs out.

But love and comfort are a long way from romance, and things have cooled slightly since that one surprise make-out session with Milo. Of course it's all reasonable, given everything that has happened, for us to put it on hold for a bit. It doesn't mean I've been any less attracted, or aware of that attraction, in the meantime. There's just been so much to deal with, I feel like I scarcely have time to come up for air before someone is shoving my head back underwater.

For their part, the guys promised they wouldn't push me, and now that I'm the alpha, I have a sneaking suspicion they're a little intimidated. My mind has been constantly rolling over the concept of having three mates, and I've brought myself to a fiery blush more than once imagining how things would… work.

But now it's the end of classes on Monday, and all that remains is English 101. I'm grateful that we're almost done—it was a long weekend, and one more class will end our day. Jared decreed that he's going to skip football practice this afternoon, and all three guys are coming to my place for a movie night immediately after. William is already planning on making his famous pizzas. Even though we just had them a few days ago, the guys can't seem to get enough.

They escort me to class in our usual configuration,

and Landon's handing me my bag when I glance up and see the back of a familiar-looking head pass through the crowd and into my classroom.

My heart immediately begins pounding, but I take a few breaths to calm myself. *There's no way.*

"Layla, is everything okay?" Landon's voice is edged with concern.

"Yeah, I'm fine. I just thought for a second I saw someone I recognized, that's all. But I realized I will probably think that for the rest of my life now," I joke feebly.

"Very true," Milo agrees, lifting my hand for a kiss. "Okay, Lex, we'll meet you out front after class." He and Landon turn and head for their class, and Jared grins. My heart pings briefly to watch them go, but I know only fifty minutes separate me from seeing them again.

"Now I've got you all to myself. Hey Layla, what did one wall say to another?" Jared gestures for me to enter the classroom and I step ahead, angling for our usual seats.

"I dunno, what?"

"I'll meet you at the corner."

I groan. "You know, I'm starting to second guess my defense of your jokes. I think they're getting worse."

"Nah, you're just tired," Jared teases with a wink.

We settle into our seats, and as the classroom quiets down, the professor clears his throat and begins to speak. Immediately, an icy sweat breaks out across my back, and I stare down at the professor's desk in shock.

"Layla, are you okay? What is it, gorgeous?" Jared, obviously sensing my distress, hisses in my ear.

But I can't reply. All I can do is stare.

It's as if I've stepped into the Twilight Zone, with my long-distant past and my new life smashing together in a bizarre wreck of a reality.

The professor continues. "I know you started the semester with Professor Johnson, but fortunately for me, he accepted a last-minute position elsewhere and this spot opened up." His eyes search through the lecture hall and land on me, holding my gaze while he smiles widely. "I'm Professor Derrek Westin, and I just moved here from California."

The End

Ready for more? Continue Layla's story in Pack Nightmare

Want a little extra? Join my newsletter and instantly get an extra scene from Pack Dreams!
http://laurelnight.com/packdreams

THE WARRIOR QUEEN LEGACY - COMPLETE SERIES

A SLOW-BURN REVERSE harem romance featuring a fantasy dystopian setting that has been compared to 'I Am Legend' crossed with 'The Shanarra Chronicles' and wolf shifters. Named one of Book Authority's Top Fantasy Books of 2021, and Red-Feather Romance's 10 Top Adult Fantasy Romances. Available on multiple retailers

SCENT OF DECEPTION - A STANDALONE IN THE BONDS OF STEELE OMEGAVERSE

Raised to be a pampered omega, Sapphire Steele never manifested. Desperate, she accepted a lucrative proposal: Pretend to be the omega for a wealthy pack until one of the alphas receives his inheritance, then disappear with her share of the money…. But someone knows her secret… Available on multiple retailers

GLAM - A STANDALONE MAFIA-LITE REVERSE HAREM ROMANCE

The hardworking daughter of two cops finally lands her dream job, only to be interrupted on her first day by three devastatingly handsome mafia brothers she recognized from college. Always out of her reach before, they're suddenly obsessed with her, and insist she become a part of their glittering world. Then, one night she witnesses first hand what happens in the back room of those shimmering parties, and how the Vargas family have ruled over Miami for decades.

Terrified, she knows with certainty that one of two things will happen: Either she becomes theirs, beholden to them and immersed in their world of wealth and privilege for the rest of her life.

Or no one will ever hear from her again. Check it out on Amazon

About the Author

LAUREL NIGHT IS a long-time fan of romance and adventure. She's traveled the world, and currently resides in the shadow of the Great Smoky Mountains with her daughter Tessa.

For more about Laurel, her books, and future projects, you can find her at www.laurelnight.com, or hanging around in Laurel's Night Queens, her group on Facebook.

If you'd like to stay up to date on Laurel's work, you can join Laurel's newsletter at

www.laurelnight.com/newsletter